THE A-TEAM VII:
BULLETS, BIKINIS AND BELLS

Grabbing her purse, Sandy stepped down from her barstool and told her sister, 'Put your shoes on, Tina. I'm afraid this has turned out to be a dead end after all.'

'I take it you're not the dancing type, then,' the newcomer said, flipping his quarter across the counter to the bartender as he eyed the women. 'I could have sworn–'

'Don't bother,' Tina huffed.

'You hardly touched your drinks,' the bartender said, holding the ten spot out to them. 'Around here, the daquiris come with a warranty. No like, no pay. . .'

'Keep it,' Sandy told him. 'We just changed our minds, that's all.'

'Sorry, but I have to insist that you take this money back,' the bartender said. 'You see, those drinks are on The A-Team.'

'What?' Sandy gasped, stopping in her tracks.

'The A-Team?' Tina said, turning back to the bar. 'Are you serious?'

'I'm not only serious,' the bartender said, 'I'm also Hannibal Smith. And this here's Templeton Peck.'

Also available in Target

THE A-TEAM
THE A-TEAM II: SMALL BUT DEADLY WARS
THE A-TEAM III: WHEN YOU COMIN' BACK,
                 RANGE RIDER?
THE A-TEAM IV: OLD SCORES TO SETTLE
THE A-TEAM V: TEN PERCENT OF TROUBLE
THE A-TEAM VI: OPERATION DESERT SUN:
                 THE UNTOLD STORY

THE A-TEAM PLOT IT YOURSELF I:
   DEFENCE AGAINST TERROR
THE A-TEAM PLOT IT YOURSELF II:
   THE DANGER MAZE

THE A-TEAM VII:
BULLETS, BIKINIS AND BELLS

A novel by Ron Renauld

Based on the television series 'The A-Team'
Created by Frank Lupo and Stephen J. Cannell
Adapted from the episodes 'Bullets and Bikinis'
written by Mark Jones, and
'The Bells of St Mary's' written by
Stephen J. Cannell

TARGET

A TARGET BOOK

published by
the Paperback Division of
W.H. ALLEN & Co. PLC

A Target Book
Published in 1985
by the Paperback Division of
W.H. Allen & Co. PLC
44 Hill Street, London W1X 8LB

The A-Team is a trademark of Stephen J. Cannell Productions
and licenced by Universal City Studios, Inc.

Phototypeset by Hart Typesetting Services, Basingstoke, Hants.
Printed and bound in Great Britain by
Anchor Brendon Ltd, Tiptree, Essex

ISBN 0 426 20157 4

Prologue

The sparrows of San Juan Capistrano have nothing on post-pubescent America when it comes to heralding the coming of spring. At the same time the tiny winged horde is flocking to the old mission in southern California, a similar gathering is taking place on the other coast, as millions of pale, party-starved teenagers and young collegians descend upon the bleached sands of Florida's coastal haunts, eager to lubricate themselves with equal parts of tanning lotion and liquid refreshment as they celebrate the end of yet another long, harsh winter and the beginning of the more frivolous pursuits that come with the first hint of warm weather. A hearty mania overtakes much of the Sunshine State's Atlantic coastline, and during the ensuing months, local merchants will patiently endure the nerve-wracking antics of their youthful clientele, taking solace in the glut of tourist dollars that end up in their coffers. Although Fort Lauderdale has garnered the widest renown as the site of this springtime phenomenon, anyone toting a picnic lunch to the beach in any other ocean-front town on the coast will be apt to find the sands thriving with bikini-clad sunbathers, muscle-bound surfers, rowdy volleyball enthusiasts, and half-crazed daredevils in dune buggies—all carrying on to the raucous beat of top ten hits blaring over dashboard speakers or portable radios with enough oomph to drive seagulls into a wild frenzy.

Miami Beach, an island resort town connected to the Florida mainland by four causeways, attracts an older, wealthier breed of visitor and resident with its sprawl of luxury hotels and lavish estates, but here and there are sections of beach and adjoining facilities catering to the descendants of old Annette Funicello-Frankie Avalon movies. One such establishment was the Surfsider Hotel, a small, one-storey building flanked on either side by taller, more prestigious counterparts. The Surfsider had been around since before Gidget's time, and the place still reeked of an old-postcard kind of charm.

Unfortunately, however, nostalgia didn't seem to be drawing crowds to the Surfsider, and business was particularly bleak at the hotel's beachfront restaurant, where only a handful of diners sat in the shade of Cinzano umbrellas and sipped Mai Tais as they waited for their shishkabob-fruit platter combos and watched the surf crowd romp in the choppy waters a mere Frisbee throw away. Young waitresses in Polynesian skirts and bikini tops padded about the patio, trying to look busy and cheerful in the face of lousy business.

Tina Conlon, the hotel's co-owner and hostess, was having a hard time hiding her feelings. Fidgeting with the collar of her blouse, she paced over to where her older sister was refilling salt shakers at the busboy's station.

'How much longer do we have to hang in here, Sandy?' Tina complained, gesturing out at the sparse crowd on the patio. 'I mean, look at this place. . . look what's happened to it.'

Sandy sighed and set down the salt container. Her nickname had come from the colour of her hair, which was several shades lighter than her sister's. She ran a hand through her bangs and took a hard look at Tina. They'd been through this discussion before, and Sandy felt like she was sounding like a broken record, but she once again stood up to Tina's pessimism. 'How long did Pop hang in there?' she asked rhetorically. 'Until he died, right, Tina? We have to keep at it, in his memory. Don't worry, we'll make it work.'

'I don't know, Sandy. You think so? I mean, really?' Tina was on the verge of tears and she grabbed for a cocktail napkin to dab her eyes. 'I'm having my doubts. . .'

'We're fighters, Tina,' Sandy said, putting her arm around her sister. 'Always remember that. You know what Pop always said. . ."When the going gets tough. . ."'

'Yeah, yeah, the tough get going.' Tina crumpled up the napkin and tossed it in the trash. Seeing two men step through the doorway leading to the patio, she grabbed two menus and told Sandy, 'Okay, I'll keep my chin up. Somehow we'll manage.'

'That's the spirit, sis!'

The two men were tall and bulky, with hardened features, like those of pro linebackers who hadn't had their daily ration of raw meat yet. They glared at Tina as she approached them, putting on a cordial smile.

'Good afternoon, gentlemen, and welcome to—'

'Who said we were gentle?' the taller of the men interrupted with a growl.

'Just an expression,' Tina replied warily. 'We should have a table for you any second. Can I take your name?'

The other man took the menus from Tina. Even though they were laminated, he had no trouble ripping them in half. 'Yeah, my name's Trouble, and you got some of it coming to ya, lady.'

Tina watched with horror as the men strode out onto the patio and tipped over the nearest table. The first man ripped out the umbrella and began cutting it up with a switchblade while his companion moved over and began demolishing a dessert cart with his bare fists.

'What are you doing?' Sandy shouted, moving to confront the men. 'Stop that! Stop it!'

One of the busboys rushed over to the men, but they were both a head taller than him, and a wicked right cross sent him tumbling into a planter box filled with succulents that snapped under his weight. The man who had

7

delivered the blow held his hand out for a high-five from his partner, then reached over and grabbed a Mai Tai from one of the customers. He swilled it down, then smashed the glass on the tiled floor as he smacked his lips.

'Hey, not bad!' he told Sandy. 'Could use a little more rum, though. Hey, Rocky, whaddya think about the drinks here?'

As Rocky, the shorter of the men, chased away a few more patrons and helped himself to a pitcher of beer, Tina drew her hands to her face and shrieked, 'Oh, my God!'

Sandy was more furious than afraid, and she rushed the men, beating futilely at them with her fists as she demanded, 'Get out of here! Get out!'

Rocky grabbed the woman from behind and pulled her away, then spun her around so they were faced off, eyeball to eyeball. 'You don't learn, do you, lady?' he seethed, shoving her to the ground. 'This place is goin' out of business, once and for all!'

'You'll pay for this!' Sandy vowed as she struggled to her feet. A slap across the face sent her back to the floor.

'Whatever you say, sweetheart,' Rocky chortled. He gulped down a few more swallows of beer, then belched loudly and tossed the pitcher through the plate glass window leading to the kitchen. With a howl, he cried out, 'Hey, now this is my idea of a happy hour, eh, Eddie?'

Eddie was sampling a chocolate cream pie he'd rescued from the dessert cart. He nodded, then rammed the pie into the face of a chef who came charging out of the kitchen, waving his spatula like a battleaxe.

By now the restaurant's patrons had fled to the beach, joining the mob of youngsters that watched the demolition of the patio with fascination. Tina rushed to her sister's side and helped Sandy to her feet. 'Let's get out of here and call the police!'

'Y-y-yeah,' Sandy muttered, still stunned from the manhandling she'd received. Her lip was bleeding where she'd struck it on a tabletop when she was shoved by Rocky. Tina gave her a napkin to press against the wound as they retreated from the patio, where Eddie was now igniting umbrellas with a cigarette lighter and Rocky was chomping down somebody's abandoned shishkabob.

'Who are they?' Tina gasped as she led her sister down the indoor hallway leading to their office. 'Why are—'

'Oh, come on, Tina,' Sandy interjected bitterly. 'A couple of brainless thugs like them have to be working for someone else. Figure it out!'

'Of course,' Tina realised. 'Joey Epic!'

The women didn't have long to wait to confirm their suspicions. When they rushed into the office, Joey Epic himself was seated behind the desk, surrounded by thriving ferns and a large-capacity fish tank filled with colourful, exotic fish. Epic was fairly colourful and exotic as well, encased in a blue, three-piece suit that seemed ready to burst from his stocky frame. His fingers glittered from rings set with a variety of precious stones, and his hair was living testimony that the wet look was not dead. Dark, rank-smelling smoke curled up from the tip of his cigar like exhaust from an engine in bad need of a tune-up.

'Hello, ladies!' he greeted them cheerfully, pointing to a set of chairs along the wall. 'Come in, have a seat.'

'What are you doing in our office?' Sandy demanded.

'Admiring the ferns,' Epic confided, the smile never leaving his face. 'Nice, healthy plants, they are. Of course, I could swear I saw them cringing from all that racket out on your patio.'

Just then, the sound of another table being overturned came through the panelled wall behind Epic, and he closed his eyes, shaking his head sadly as he puffed his cigar.

'It's an outrage!' Sandy declared, still dabbing at her lip as she leaned across the desk and stared at Epic. 'Do you hear me? We won't tolerate it!'

'I can't say as I blame you,' Epic said calmly. 'Tables tipping over. Busboys getting hit and what not. That kind of mayhem can be real bad for business, I'll bet. Maybe you should call the police, hmm?'

As Epic picked up the phone and started dialling a number, Sandy pointed to the door behind her and told the man, 'Get the hell off our property!'

Ignoring the command, Epic finished dialling and cupped his hand over the mouthpiece, telling the women, 'I have a friend in the police department. Sergeant Morgan. We grew up together. I'll be happy to see what he can do for you girls.'

Sandy grabbed Joey's wrist and jerked it down sharply so that the receiver slammed back onto the phone cradle. 'You're dirt, Joey!' she shouted contemptuously. 'And I don't care what strong arm tactics you want to try, you're not getting this hotel!'

Epic pulled his hand away from Sandy and realigned his rings, then reached calmly for a framed photograph of the two women with an older man who bore a striking resemblance to them. 'You know,' he reflected, 'you two are just as stubborn as your old man was. He didn't want to sell this hotel, either.'

'And he went to his grave fighting you, you greedy little vermin!' Sandy snatched the photo away from Epic.

Tina, trembling with fear, stepped up behind her sister and pleaded with Epic, 'Please, just leave us alone.'

'Don't you dare stoop to begging,' Sandy told her sister. Pointing a warning finger at Epic, she added, 'I won't tell you again. Get off this property and take your gorillas with you!'

Joey shrugged his shoulders complacently and stood up. He blew smoke and sighed, 'You had a real nice hotel here. A real nice place.' He turned his attention to the fish tank and went on, 'These fish are real nice, too. Real pretty and delicate. Just like the two of you. It'd be a shame to have to hurt such lovely creatures. . .'

Epic suddenly raised the lid of the tank and jabbed his cigar into the water. Black soot began to spread out, sending the fish scattering frantically. As the girls stared at this latest act of desecration, Epic moved out from behind the desk and silently left the room.

1

Three days and twenty-seven hundred miles later, the
Conlon sisters staggered wearily into the fan-cooled
refuge of a hole-in-the-wall tavern servicing the small
town of Palmdale, California, located a half-hour's drive
north-east of Los Angeles. Dust from the desert had
covered their rental car and clung to their wilted dresses,
which were showing the effects of their day-long wild-
goose chase throughout various parts of the teeming
metropolis. A sweltering heat wave hadn't done wonders
for either of the women's jet lag, and as they slumped
down on bar stools, they ignored the roving eyes of
flyboys from the nearby Air Force base and other
backroad Romeos intrigued by the arrival of newcomers.

'My feet are killing me,' Tina groaned, slipping out of
her sandals and wriggling her toes in the air. 'All day
we've been getting the runaround, and now that Mr Lee
guy sends us out to the boonies and says that *maybe*
there's an outside chance this hotshot A-Team might
decide to show their faces. I tell you, sis, this is sounding
more and more like a scam all the time.'

Sandy checked a message on a small scrap of paper,
comparing instructions with the name of the bar posted
above the liquor racks to make sure they'd come to the right

place. She was as wary as her sister, and when she began to note the leering glances being cast her way, she too wondered if she'd been led astray by an acquaintance back in Miami Beach who had suggested the The A-Team might be worth looking into. She tried to hide her concern, though, and assured Tina, 'It's the only shot we have. Besides, we didn't come all the way to Los Angeles to give up now.'

'I could have guessed you'd say that,' Tina said, forcing a smile. 'If there's one thing my big sister will always have over me, it's stubbornness.'

'I like to think of it more as determination,' Sandy countered, brushing back her hair and leaning for support on the counter.

As someone fed quarters to the jukebox and filled the bar with a string of woeful country laments, the bartender, a balding man with a bushy moustache, sauntered over to the women and drawled, 'What'll it be, ladies?'

'How about a foot massage?' Tina sighed.

'Or a of couple daquiris,' Sandy said.

'Daquiris I have,' the bartender told them, pulling down a couple of glasses from the overhead rack next to him. 'I can't help you on the massage front, though. Health codes, you know. Of course, I'm sure if you look around, you'll find your share of willing volunteers.'

'Tell me about it.' Sandy glanced over her shoulder, noticing a man watching her from the pool table, grinning with a mouth short on teeth. She looked away from him and took in the others at the bar, finding none that looked like the men Mr Lee had mentioned when they had met him in Chinatown earlier that morning.

'This looks like the kind of place I'd come to looking for trouble instead of help,' Tina whispered, leaning close to her sister. 'It's creepy.'

As he mixed their drinks, the bartender kept his eyes on the women. 'You know, people say bartenders are better than psychiatrists at reading people.' He paused long enough to garnish the daquiris, then set the drinks before the sisters, adding, 'You two look like you have a lot on your minds.'

12

Tina rolled her eyes, having reached her limit. 'Look, pal,' she advised the bartender, 'my sister and I are really tired and not in the mood for a lot of idle chatter, so could we just have our drinks without the psychology?'

'Tina,' Sandy said, putting a hand on her sister's arm. 'Take it easy. . .'

'Yeah,' the bartender said, filling a small basket with complimentary pretzels and passing it to the women. 'I was just trying to be friendly is all. . .'

'Thank you,' Sandy replied, plucking up a pretzel.

Tina took a sip from her drink, then set it down and apologized to the bartender. 'I'm sorry. It's just that. . . well it's a long story. I won't bother going into it. Let's just say we've had a rough day.'

'Is there any other kind?' The bartender ignored the ten dollar bill Sandy had placed on the counter and went over to the old Zenith television perched on a suspended platform near the end of the bar. He switched it on, and when the black-and-white image refused to settle into focus, he beat on the side of the set with his fist. The picture got worse. Shrugging his shoulder, the bartender raised his voice and called out to the patrons, 'Tube's on the fritz again, boys. If you wanna catch the fight, you'll have to try over at Carol's place. Sorry. . .'

There were assorted grumbles as half the people in the tavern quickly finished their drinks and began filing toward the door. The bartender waved to those who bothered to look his way.

'When you gonna get that TV fixed?' the gap-toothed pool player whined.

'Soon as we raise the price of drinks, we'll bring in one of them fancy, big-screened jobbers,' the bartender promised.

'Forget it,' the pool player said on his way out the door.

As the bartender headed back toward the women, Sandy raised a hand to get his attention, then asked, 'Listen, did anyone by any chance leave a message for Tina or Sandy?'

'I just came on,' the bartender revealed. He checked a

13

small pegboard next to the cash register. 'Doesn't look like anybody left any notes or anything, though.'

'Okay, just checking.' Sandy wrapped her fingers around the coolness of her glass, then dabbed her forehead with her hand. 'Thanks, anyway.'

'No problem.' As he started gathering up empty pitchers and beer mugs, the bartender told the women, 'You two have interesting accents. I bet you're from Jacksonville, right?'

'Right state, wrong city,' Sandy replied. 'We're from Miami Beach. Say are you this curious about all of your clients?'

Before the bartender could answer, another man strolled up to the women and flashed a lady-killer smile. Unlike most of the other bar patrons, he was dressed like someone from the city, wearing a designer shirt and slacks along with Gucci loafers. 'Hi, there,' he said, holding up a quarter. 'I've got two bits that says somewhere on that jukebox is a song that'll make one of you fine ladies want to dance. How about it?'

It was Sandy's turn to roll her eyes. Grabbing her purse, she stepped down from her barstool and told her sister, 'Put your shoes on, Tina. I'm afraid this has turned out to be a dead end after all.'

'I take it you're not the dancing type, then,' the newcomer said, flipping his quarter across the counter to the bartender as he eyed the women. 'I could have sworn—'

'Don't bother,' Tina huffed.

'You hardly touched your drinks,' the bartender said, holding the ten spot out to them. 'Around here, the daquiris come with a warranty. No like, no pay. . .'

'Keep it,' Sandy told him. 'We just changed our minds, that's all.'

'Sorry, but I have to insist that you take this money back,' the bartender said. 'You see, those drinks are on The A-Team.'

'What?' Sandy gasped, stopping in her tracks.

'The A-Team?' Tina said, turning back to the bar. 'Are you serious?'

14

'I'm not only serious,' the bartender said, tugging the moustache from his upper lip and removing the bald wig covering his full head of silver hair. 'I'm also Hannibal Smith. And this here's Templeton Peck.'

Peck took the drink Hannibal had just given him and hoisted it in the air as he addressed the women. 'You can call me Face.'

Seeing the two men in a new light, Sandy grinned for the first time since arriving in Los Angeles. 'Of course! I should have suspected. Sorry we were so rude, but we thought that you were—'

'That's quite all right,' Hannibal interjected, moving out from behind the bar. 'We don't like having to subject any potential clients to this kind of runaround, but you have to understand our position. We needed to check you out.'

'And you checked out rather nicely,' Face confirmed between sips of his drink.

Tina blushed at the flattery while Hannibal explained further, 'We just wanted to be sure you stayed with the same story you told Mister Lee and that you weren't being followed by certain people who have it in for us. Can't be too careful, you know.'

'I guess not,' Sandy said, gesturing at the now-deserted bar. 'This is definitely an out-of-the-way spot.'

'You like it?' Hannibal said. 'We own a slice of it.'

Face stared over the rim of his drink, reflecting, 'It was payment for an assignment in which we had to smuggle some Senator's son out of a political prison in Cyprus. We always wanted a place away from the city where we could hide out when the heat got to be too much in LA, in both senses of the word. It has a nice, down-home atmosphere, don't you think?'

'I suppose you could say that,' Tina said. 'But aren't there four of you on the Team?'

Hannibal went to the front door, putting up a 'CLOSED' sign before throwing the deadbolt. As he led the others to the back exit, he told the Conlon sisters, 'Yeah, but our associate Murdock is currently back in the Veterans'

Hospital for his annual ink blot exam. B.A.'s down there springing him for a quick vacation. If your problem's as severe as you make it out to be, we'll want to bring in the whole team.'

'That's a relief,' Tina said.

'Besides,' Face added, 'we get tired of the Pacific and thought it'd be nice to check out the beaches on the other coast.'

'If you can help us, we'll be glad to let you stay at our hotel and use the beach as much as you want,' Sandy offered.

'We don't come quite that cheaply,' Hannibal said, 'but I'm sure we'll be able to work something out.'

Outside, sundown had lowered the temperature slightly, and a gentle breeze stirred the trees in the parking lot. As the foursome piled into the women's rental car, Tina asked Face 'What's wrong with Mr Murdock that would put him in the Vets' hospital?'

'You'll find out soon enough,' Face promised.

2

Murdock had been in and out of the Veterans' Hospital in West Los Angeles so many times in recent years that patients and staff members alike had begun calling him Yo-Yo. He didn't like the tag, feeling that it lacked the verve and pizzaz of his longstanding nickname, Howling Mad, which he'd earned during his exploits as a chopper pilot in Viet Nam. When B.A. showed up at his room in the observation ward, meagrely disguised as a medical officer in green togs and matching surgeon's cap, Murdock couldn't wait to vent his displeasure.

'They're calling me Yo-Yo, B.A.,' he whined, clutching at the sleeve of B.A.'s uniform. 'It's not right! I'm so much more than a string toy!'

B.A. glanced over his shoulder to make sure the nurse in the doorway hadn't overheard, then leaned close to Murdock and hissed, 'Shut your face and lemme get you outta here or they're gonna be calling you Basket Case.'

'Basket Case. . . Basket Case,' Murdock sounded out the name, trying it on for size. He finally shook his head. 'Nah, I don't like that one, either.'

B.A. grunted with disgust and produced a roll of gauze from his pocket. Before Murdock could react, B.A. was gagging him and calling out to the nurse, 'I think we need to use the straitjacket, too. No telling how he'll react to the serum.'

As Murdock protested ineffectively through the gag, B.A. pinned his associate down on the bed long enough for the nurse and an orderly to bind Murdock with the straitjacket.

'I certainly hope this serum works,' the nurse told B.A., 'Mr Murdock's been extremely agitated lately.'

'That's a fact,' the orderly put in. 'Ol' Yo-Yo's been even weirder than usual.'

'Mmmmmummpffff!' Murdock screamed at the orderly, wriggling out of B.A.'s grasp and lunging to his feet. B.A. quickly grabbed Murdock and slammed him into the wheelchair the orderly had wheeled into the room.

'I think we ought to give him the injection right now,' B.A. said, giving Murdock's shoulder a squeeze that rivalled the Vulcan Death Grip in rendering its victim helpless. Murdock contorted his face into an expression of anguish that lasted until the nurse had driven home the syringe B.A. had brought to the hospital along with his bogus papers authorising the injection.

'I still can't believe they've come up with this serum,' the nurse said as she swabbed clean the spot where she'd given Murdock the shot, then applied a bandage. 'To think that it might be able to totally suppress all symptoms of paranoid schizophrenia. . . why, the implications are staggering! You could be up for a Nobel Prize for this, doctor!'

'Just helping people like this is reward enough for me,' B.A. confided, taking up position behind the wheelchair and starting to roll Murdock out of the room. 'Of course, we won't know for sure about how it's working on him until we've had him under observation for a few days. Did you get his release papers signed?'

'Yes I did,' the nurse said, producing a clipboard with the forged sheets in question. She gave the pages to B.A. as she and the orderly walked alongside the wheelchair.

'We're used to Yo-Yo being released and readmitted,' the orderly joked. 'We could almost come up with a rubber stamp to cut through all the red tape.'

Murdock glared at the orderly and tried to live up to his

original nickname, but the gauze muffled his howling considerably. He strained at the binds of the straitjacket until B.A. discreetly snapped one of his ringed fingers against the base of Murdock's skull. Murdock went rigid for a moment, then slumped limply back in the chair the rest of the way out of the hospital.

'The serum must be taking effect,' B.A. said. 'I shouldn't have any more problems with him. Thanks for all your assistance.'

'Glad to help,' the nurse said. 'If everything works out, it will have been an honour to have been part of the experiment.'

The orderly held the front door open for B.A., and as Murdock was being wheeled out, he called out, 'Good luck, Yo-Yo!'

Murdock swung his head around, flashing the orderly the evil eye as B.A. guided the wheelchair down the handicapped ramp leading to the parking lot, where The A-Team van was parked. A special emblem decal had been applied to the sides of the vehicle, declaring it to be property of the Veterans' Administration's Medical Investigations branch.

Once B.A. had helped Murdock up into the back of the van, he ungagged him and growled, 'Don't say I never did you any favours, fool!'

'Go ahead, call me Fool!' Murdock said appreciatively, rubbing his chin against his shoulder. 'Anything but Yo-Yo!'

'Anything?'

'Well. . .' When B.A. closed the back door behind him and moved up to the driver's seat, Murdock cried, 'Hey, wait a sec, big guy. What about this straitjacket?'

'What about it?' B.A. said, grinning back at Murdock in the rearview mirror. 'I gotta drive to meet the others. I can't keep an eye on you at the same time.'

'But what's the need?' Murdock said. 'I feel great, B.A.! I don't know what was in that shot, but, hey, it worked like a charm! I'm sane, big guy. Let me out of this cocoon, okay?'

B.A. started up the engine. 'That shot wasn't nothin'

but vitamins and glucose, man! You're still crazy as a nut bar and I ain't lettin' you loose until Hannibal or Face is back there to keep you in line.'

'Rude, B.A., very rude.' Murdock stared out the front window as the van rolled out of the parking lot and onto the streets. 'I'm tellin' ya, that shot did something to me and. . . ohhhhhh.'

'What now, fool?' B.A. called out over his shoulder, hearing the groan coming from the back seat.

'Jekyll? Jekyll!? Did you say my name was Jekyll?' Murdock intoned dramatically. His eyes drew wide in wonder, then screwed themselves tight as Murdock sucked in his cheeks and cackled in a strange voice, 'Nay, 'tis Hyde! Oh, the serum! The serum! I'm changing, changing. . .'

B.A. shook his head and got onto the freeway, picking up speed in the van. 'Man, why did I take off his gag? I oughta have *my* head examined!'

As it was, B.A.'s head was in need of examination, but for another reason. In recent days, a growing pain had been plaguing one of his teeth, and as he sped up to pass a truck and reflexively grit his jaw, the dull ache came to furious life inside his mouth.

'Yeowwwwww!' B.A. grimaced.

'You're in pain?' Murdock questioned, becoming strangely calm now and knowing, 'Tell me where it hurts, my good man. I'm a doctor. I can help you. Jekyll's the name. . .'

'You're the worse pain I got to deal with, sucker!' B.A. snarled, massaging his jaw until the throbbing subsided. 'You better shake this Jekyll and Hyde jive before we meet up with the ladies Hannibal and Face are sizin' up. They ain't gonna hire no team with a whacko on it!'

'Whacko?' Murdock writhed against the grip of his straitjacket, then began to grin menacingly. 'I'm not a whacko, heh heh. Not a whacko, not a yo-yo, but Hyde. . . Aaaaargh! Look! My hands! See the hair growing, the fingers bending to claws? Ohhhhh, what a world! Serum! I need more serum!'

B.A. swerved sharply to his right and pulled to a stop on the freeway's shoulder. Turning around in his seat, he waved a ring-encrusted fist a few inches away from Murdock's face. 'This is a special serum for fools like you, Murdock! How many doses do you want?'

Murdock shrank away from the fist, offering B.A. a frail smile. 'Awwww, come on, big guy. I'm just having a little fun playing out our charade, that's all. You know as well as me that I'm playing with a full deck.'

B.A. slowly pulled his fist away, still suspicious. 'On the level? No more crazy business?'

'Absolutely,' Murdock promised, quickly adding, 'on the condition that you let me out of this straitjacket. I mean, you're the one who said the ladies might be upset to see an alleged whacko in their midst, eh, B.A.?'

B.A. put the van back into gear and waited for traffic to clear, then floored the accelerator and got back on the freeway, leaving Murdock immobilised. 'You almost had me, man,' he said, 'But I been around you too long. I let you outta that straitjacket and I'll regret it.'

Before Murdock could protest further, B.A. cranked up the volume on the van's radio and turned his full attention to the traffic on the freeway. In the back, Murdock stewed in his frustration, muttering to himself, 'With stoic silence, Howling Mad Murdock endured the abuses heaped on him, knowing that soon his moment would come, and the world would take notice and know that here was a man who gave new meaning to the word brilliant. . . heh heh heh. . . brink on zee fräuleins, Herr Baracus. Zey vill find me most intriguing. . .'

3

The A-Team had arranged to rendezvous in the parking lot of a small shopping centre on Ventura Boulevard in the Encino area of the San Fernando Valley. B.A. and Murdock pulled into the lot early, finding most of the activity to be centred around an ice cream emporium that served as a hangout for high schoolers who looked and sounded like escapees from the song 'Valley Girl'.

'You stay here, sucker,' B.A. warned Murdock as he got out of the van. 'I gotta hit the drug store and get something for my tooth. Keep an eye open for Hannibal and Face.'

Murdock said nothing, but the sinister glint in his eyes betrayed nefarious intent. He waited until he saw B.A. disappear inside the pharmacy, then inched his way to the front of the van. With considerable difficulty, he was able to pry one foot free of his shoe. Sniggering with glee, he raised his leg and used his loose toes to raise the lock knob and then open the passenger's door.

'Ha ha!' he gloated triumphantly as he slithered out of the van, 'They thought they'd tanned this Hyde, but he was not one to be so easily thwarted. No sir, here was a consummate—'

'Hey, check out that dude!' one of the teenage boys

cried out from the nearby curb in front of the ice cream stand.

'Like, far out!' the youth's girlfriend gushed between laps at her double-decker cone. 'Hey, mister, like, where'd you cop those bitchin' threads?'

Murdock froze in place, realizing how conspicuous he looked in his straitjacket, baggy slacks, one shoe and baseball cap. However, once he had a good look at the teenagers watching him, he realised that, if anything, he was dressed conservatively. The youths loitering by the ice cream stand wore dated *Flashdance* fashions and hairdos that looked as if they'd been executed with hedge shears and food colouring. One of the boys had a portable radio, and he slapped in a particularly raucous cassette, filling the parking lot with a jackhammer drum beat.

'Dance to that, dude!' he called out to Murdock.

As the youths started moving toward him, Murdock blanched with fear and staggered hurriedly into the refuge of the pharmacy. Spotting B.A. at the cash counter, he rushed over and began pleading with the pharmacist ringing up the sale.

'Serum, kind sir! I beg you! Have pity on this poor frantic schizophrenic! Pleeeeeease! I need another reality!'

The pharmacist recoiled from the register and put his hands up so quickly that he knocked his bifocals from his nose and sent them clattering onto the countertop. 'I just made a deposit, but you can have what's here. Just don't shoot. I'm a grandfather!'

B.A. tossed a couple of dollars on the counter to pay for the extract of cloves the pharmacist had given him for his toothache, assuring the grey-haired man, 'Don't worry, this fool won't hurt you. Ain't that right, Murdock?'

'Serum, that's all I ask of you,' Murdock implored.

B.A. slipped the pharmacist another bill and grabbed a couple of golf ball-sized jawbreakers from a display jar next to the register. 'Here, two of these should do the trick!' he told Murdock, popping the candies in his partner's mouth and filling out his cheeks so he looked like a chipmunk hoarding foodstuffs for the winter.

'Mammmrrrffffpooooooffff!' Murdock blabbed as B.A. grabbed a strap of the straitjacket and led him out of the store. Outside, the Valley kids had gathered around the van, but when they spotted B.A. they quickly backtracked. Noticing the clutter of gold jewelry hanging from his neck and arms, one of the boys pointed and cried out, 'Oh, man, the dude's gotta be into heavy metal. Barf me out!'

'I'll do more than barf you out if you don't get away from my wheels, man!' B.A. warned. He sneered to add emphasis to his warning and promptly winced from a new blast of pain generating from his rebel tooth. As the teenagers scattered, B.A. ushered a drooling Murdock back into the van, then dabbed a drop of the cloves extract onto his fingertip and rubbed it against his belligerent gums until the aching subsided. By the time he'd had a chance to circle around, the Conlon sisters' rental car pulled into the parking lot and came to a halt next to the van.

As Hannibal and Face introduced the women to the rest of the team, Murdock continued to suck on his jawbreakers, trying to melt them down to the point where he could speak coherently. Sandy and Tina weren't sure if Murdock or B.A. made them feel the most uneasy. Hannibal noted their apprehension, and as he held the door open for the women to get inside the van, he told them, 'Don't go by appearances. B.A. and Murdock are both crack commandoes, and when the going gets tough—'

'They get going,' Sandy said with a laugh. 'Funny, but I could swear I've heard that saying somewhere before.'

Once everyone was piled into the van, B.A. pulled out and headed back into the hills south of the Boulevard, where The A-Team had been staying recently at the home of an old client who was currently on an extended vacation in France. It was a cool quiet night, and a hint of jasmine filled the air. As Hannibal quickly briefed B.A. and Murdock on the background to the plight of the Conlon sisters, Face liberated Murdock from his straitjacket. Once his arms were free, Murdock shook them at his sides like a young bird testing its wings. The jawbreakers were now as small as marbles, and he was able to speak around them, his voice brimming with an excitement that had more to do with his recent sugar intake than anything else.

'I don't believe it!' he wailed, 'Two sweet, innocent girls terrorised by a sewer rat! Scum! A slime bait!'

'Slime bait?' Face placed a hand on Murdock's shoulder and told him, 'Relax, Murdock. We don't want to have to put the jacket back on, do we?'

'I'm okay, Face, honest' Murdock said, gulping down the remnants of his candies. 'You know me. . . I just get to bracing at the bit when I haven't seen action for awhile. Too much time in the rubber-walled cubicle is not good for the soul.'

Getting back to matters at hand, Sandy picked up where Hannibal had left off. 'This guy, Joey Epic, will do anything to get our hotel. He's offered to pay twice what the Surfsider is worth, and when we didn't sell, he sent his goons over to beat up our help and scare our customers away. He's doing anything he can to put us out of business and we're already two months behind on our mortgage.'

'He already owns a huge hotel called the Sunset,' Tina added, 'Not to mention half the resort city and a brand new high-rise he just had built down the street from us.'

'If he's got all that fancy real estate,' B.A. asked, 'why would he want to bother with a little place like yours in the first place?'

'That's what we can't figure,' Tina confessed. 'Whatever the reason, he wants it badly enough to pull all the stops in trying to get it.'

B.A. pulled off the main road and started down a winding thoroughfare that ran past a number of fancy-looking homes built against the hillside. A dog trotted out to the end of the driveway and barked at the van as it rolled past.

'I'm curious,' Hannibal said, unwrapping the cellophane from one of his coveted cigars. 'If he offered you so much money, why didn't you just sell and be done with all the hassles?'

'The hotel is all we have,' Tina explained. 'Our father

died a few months ago from a heart attack. We know it was from the strain Joey was putting him through. There's no way we'd ever back down and give in now.'

Once he'd turned into the lot where The A-Team was staying, B.A. pounded an angry fist on the steering wheel and said, 'Man, I'd like to take that Joey jerk and teach him to breathe underwater! One thing I can't stand and that's. . .owwwwwwwww!'

Hannibal saw B.A. grab for his jaw and asked, 'Is that tooth still acting up on you?'

'No, ain't nothin' wrong with my tooth!' B.A. lied, not wanting to show any sign of weakness in the presence of the women. It was a feeble cover-up, though, and when the tooth continued to bother him, he moaned again.

'It's those candy bars you're always snacking on, B.A.,' Face said, moving up to the front of the van and motioning for B.A. to open his mouth. 'Let's have a look.'

'Forget it, man!' B.A. slipped out of the van and headed for the house, a two-storey redwood structure half-hidden under the leafy branches of an old mulberry tree.

'Don't worry about him,' Face told the Conlon sisters as they all climbed out and headed up the walk to the front door. 'Deep down he's gentle as a lamb. Truly a sensitive guy.'

Hannibal lit up his cigar and blew a cloud of smoke into the night air as he walked. 'Well, ladies,' he divulged, 'it seems to me you've got a problem that needs looking into, and we're just the guys to do it. However, it could be expensive.'

'We have a way to pay you,' Sandy answered quickly. 'We'll sign the hotel over to you.'

'What?' Face and Hannibal murmured, 'another profit-sharing plan. . . Excuse me, ladies, but I think my associates and I will have to put our heads together on this one.'

As the sisters remained on the front steps, The A-Team huddled under the mulberry tree. B.A. hung back from the others, applying more clove extract to his tender tooth.

26

'Well, I don't know about you guys,' Face said, 'but I haven't exactly had a vacation in awhile and this sounds like just the ticket I've been looking for. A quaint hotel on the beach, miles from Decker and all those military police. . . young girls frolicking under the bright sun, just waiting for someone to sweep them off their feet. How can we miss?'

'Vacation!' Murdock's eyes lit up at the word. 'Yes, that's exactly what this tortured psyche needs. A furlough, a breather, some prime rest and relaxation!'

'Don't forget that it won't be all fun and games,' Hannibal reminded the others. 'There's the matter of dealing with Joey Epic.'

'Chump change,' B.A. said. 'He might be able to bully a couple young women, but once he tangles with the Team, he'll be singin' a different tune.'

'A tune,' Murdock chimed, still wallowing in his dreams of a soul-soothing vacation. He began to sing,

> *'We're goin' to Surf City,*
> *'cause it's two to one.*
> *We're goin' to Surf City,*
> *Gonna have some fun.*
> *Two girls for every*
> *Two girls for every*
> *Two girls for everyyyyyy—'*

'Shut up, fool, or I'll wrap that straitjacket around your face!' B.A. warned.

'Well, I think it's settled then,' Hannibal said. Breaking up the huddle, he headed for the sisters, 'Okay, ladies, you have yourselves a deal. Now, let's have some supper, then B.A.'ll take you back to your car so you can catch a flight back to Miami. We'll be there tomorrow.'

'Tomorrow!' B.A. hollered in protest. 'Hannibal, Florida's three days away by car, at least! And you know I ain't goin' up in no airplane!'

The sisters were put off by B.A.'s sudden outburst, but Hannibal hurriedly told them, 'Nothing to worry about. . . just a little domestic misunderstanding.'

'Misunderstanding nothin'!' B.A. said. 'I ain't goin' on

no airplane, and that's final!'

'I know, B.A., I know,' Hannibal said calmly. 'But if you drive three days cross country with a bad tooth you'll be no good to anybody. Tell you what. You get your tooth fixed while Face and I fly out, then you can drive out later with Murdock and meet up with us. Okay?'

'I hate dentists,' B.A. griped. 'And Murdock's crazy. No way am I gonna drive from here to Florida listenin' to his jive.'

'Well, you're going to have to take your pick, B.A.,' Hannibal said. 'Flying with us or driving with Murdock.'

B.A. rubbed his jaw, clearly displeased with his options.

'Look, B.A.,' Face offered, 'I know this great dentist. He's a close personal friend of mine. He'll take care of you in nothing flat, and I guarantee, you won't feel a thing. . .'

4

During the years that Templeton Peck had grown up in an orphanage, his dental needs had been taken care of at the offices of a charity medical group located in the north end of the Valley, near the Devonshire Downs Fairgrounds. It was an old building, covered with creeping fig and sheltered from the sun by a row of cypress pines that had merged limbs years ago to create a large wall of evergreen. Inside, the walls were papered with cartoons, and the dentist's office was filled with toys and a large aquarium filled with goldfish the size of silver dollars. When Face led B.A. into the room, the musclebound patient suddenly stopped.

'Hey, man, this is a kid's place!' he complained.

'What did you expect?' Face said as he waved to the receptionist and shoved B.A. gently in the direction of a dwarf sofa cluttered with the back issues of Scholastic magazine and a few stray tinkertoys. 'Go on, have a seat.'

'I ain't seein' no kid's dentist,' B.A. declared, crossing his arms defiantly and refusing to sit down.

'Come on, B.A., teeth are teeth, for cryin' out loud.'

Just then a pulse of pain banged at the root of B.A.'s problem tooth, and he slumped onto the sofa in misery, cradling his chin in his hand. 'All right, but he better do a good job or there's gonna be trouble.'

'Relax, would you?' Face patted B.A. reassuringly on the shoulder. 'Dentists are our friends. And just think, if you're real good and don't cry, maybe he'll give you a sucker when he's done.'

'A sucker's what I am for being here,' B.A. grumbled, flicking a tinkertoy across the room.

'Now, is that any way to act?' Face scolded. 'What if there were some children here now watching you do that? What would they think?'

'Who cares?' B.A. jutted his lower lip out, pouting.

The door to the examination rooms opened and a tall black nurse poked her head out, calling, 'Mr Baracus?'

B.A. pretended he hadn't heard his name and quickly buried his face in one of the children's magazines so he wouldn't have to face the nurse. Face smiled patiently at the woman and pointed to the cowering figure beside him. The nurse repeated B.A.'s name, and when he looked up and saw the statuesque beauty staring at him, he underwent a quick transformation. Dropping the magazine, he sat upright and beamed confidently at the woman.

'That's me!'

'Right this way, please.'

As B.A. rose to his feet, Face gave him an encouraging pat on the back. 'Go get 'em, tiger!'

B.A. brushed Face's arm away and sauntered to the back doorway, trying not to show either his anxiety or pain. The nurse continued to smile at him as she held the door open. As B.A. walked past her, she asked, 'You're not afraid, are you?'

'Me!' B.A. laughed away the very thought. 'No, ma'am, I ain't afraid of nothin'!'

'Mind if I tag along?' Face asked the nurse. 'I haven't seen ol' Doc Kalalau since my last check-up.'

'Fine, but try not to get in the way,' the nurse said. As she led B.A. to one of the rooms, she told him, 'From what we were told over the phone about your tooth, it sounds like we'll have to take it out. But don't worry, it won't hurt, because we'll put you under sedation during

30

the procedure. Okay?'

'I don't need no sedative!' B.A. boasted, sliding into the dentist's chair in the first room they came to. 'Just pull away and get it done with. I can take a little pain.'

'Let's see about that, okay?' The nurse reached for a gleaming dental tool and told B.A., 'Open wide.'

B.A. stared at the pointed tip of the instrument and swallowed hard. Perspiration was starting to bead up above his eyebrows. 'What are you going to do with that?' he asked, his voice coming out raspy from the sudden dryness in his throat.

'I'll just poke around back there and see if I can pinpoint where it hurts.'

The moment the tool was in B.A.'s mouth, he panicked and his right leg shot out at an angle, connecting with a tray filled with other instruments. The tray went flying, sending the tools in all directions.

'Sorry,' B.A. apologised sheepishly when the nurse backed away from him. 'Maybe. . . maybe I'll take some of that sedation after all. Just enough to kill the pain, mind you.'

'Oh, of course, Mr Baracus.' The nurse put away her tool and adjusted the chair so B.A. was laying at more of a horizontal angle. 'Now, just try to relax while I go get the doctor. Okay?'

B.A. nodded, but as soon as the nurse was out of the room, his fingers clenched tightly around the armrests of the chair. Face noticed and came over. 'B.A., you're tense. That's not good. Just try to think of relaxing things. You know, close your eyes and kinda drift off like you're daydreaming.'

'I don't know, man. . .'

'Try it, B.A.,' Face coached. When B.A. finally complied and lowered his eyelids, he continued, 'Okay, now think about something very calming. Like sunny days on the beaches of Florida. . .'

'The beach. . .' B.A. whispered, 'warm sand, some nice ladies.'

'Like your nurse. . .'

'Like my nurse,' B.A. agreed, smiling without opening

31

his eyes. Face looked to the doorway, where Hannibal stood, wearing a white uniform and an old-style reflector light on his head like a dimestore crown. On a signal from Face, Hannibal hurried silently into the room, reaching for the facemask connected to a cannister of knockout gas.

'You're lounging around a hotel,' Face droned in B.A.'s ear, 'sipping pina coladas and enjoying the finest cuisine. . .'

'No fruity drinks,' B.A. protested mildly, stirring in his seat. He was about to open his eyes when Hannibal quickly applied the facemask.

'Okay,' Face improvised quickly, 'Instead of pina coladas, you're sipping a nice, cold beer. . .'

As the gas began to seep from the cannister and out through the facemask, B.A. grinned dreamily and muttered, 'Yeahhhhhhh. . .'

Not sure if B.A. was out yet, Face tested him, saying, 'All of a sudden, nine millimetre dum dum bullets start eating up the palm trees all around you. Stinger missiles blow up the beach and tanks start rolling out of the sea. . .'

Beneath the mask, B.A. began to snore, a beatific smile still plastered across his face.

'He's out cold,' Hannibal pronounced, turning off the gas. 'Good job, Face.'

'Nothing to it,' Face said.

The nurse returned to the room, pushing a wheelchair in front of her. As Hannibal and Face carefully transferred the sleeping giant, she eyed B.A. with a warm smile. 'Just like a baby. Take care of him. . . and give him my phone number when he wakes, will you?'

'I think that can be arranged, nurse,' Hannibal said as he strapped B.A. into the wheelchair so he wouldn't topple forward in his sleep.

'And give our thanks to Dr Kalalau,' Face said, 'Tell him I'll definitely be in next year for that check-up.'

'You've been telling him that for the past four years,' the nurse reminded Face.

'I like to build up the suspense,' Face said.

5

B.A.'s dental appointment had been early in the morning, leaving The A-Team with plenty of time to catch a pre-noon flight out of L.A. International and arrive in Miami a few hours before sunset. Lugging B.A.'s inert mass around created an occasional delay and a need to respond to questions from various authorities along the way, but finally the Team pulled up to the Surfsider Hotel in a rental station wagon. Everyone's body clock was still a little out of touch with the new time zone, but, aside from B.A., no one seemed any worse for wear from the whirlwind jaunt from coast to coast.

Murdock was the first one out of the wagon, looking like some slightly demented poster child for the Florida Tourist Council. His Bermuda shorts clashed wildly with the colours of his Hawaiian print shirt, and he wore nearly as much camera equipment around his neck as B.A. wore jewellery. In place of his usual ball cap he was hiding his receding hairline beneath a wide-brimmed straw hat, and his pale, spindly legs led down to a pair of oversized sandals that slapped his soles with a sound like weak applause with each step he took.

'Oh, wow! This is boffo! Keen!' As he continued to ladle out expressions he'd memorised from reruns of

Dobie Gillis, Murdock raised his Polaroid and clicked the shutter release like a gunslinger polishing off a streetful of villains. The camera went through its whirring motions, but since it had no film, no pictures ever rolled out the slot beneath the lens. If Murdock was aware of the Polaroid's deficiencies, they didn't seem to bother him. As he'd explained earlier, a vacation was just the tonic he'd been hungry for, and aside from his childish exuberance, it seemed that he had succeeded in leaving his entourage of alter egos and split personalities back in Los Angeles.

Hannibal and Face went to the rear of the station wagon and removed their own luggage, but left the pieces belonging to Murdock and B.A. in place. Hannibal paused a moment to eye the hotel's front façade, a funky, outdated bit of kitsch, heavy on the neon and low on aesthetic subtlety. There was a vacancy sign posted in the office window, blinking on and off. Sandy looked out the window and waved excitedly when she spotted the Team.

'The Surfsider Hotel,' Hannibal said, reading over the sign again. 'It's got a nice ring to it. I like it.'

'That's good, since we're going to be running the place,' Face said. 'And I hate to spoil everybody's good time, but I think B.A.'s starting to come to.'

Hannibal glanced at the passenger's side of the front seat, where B.A. was strapped in place with his shoulder strap and seat belt, snoring fitfully out one side of his mouth and periodically shifting his position and grunting. 'Okay, gang. It's time to make plan A come together. . .'

Fortunately, the station wagon had bench seats, so Murdock and Face were able to drag B.A. from where he was sitting and place him in position behind the steering wheel. Once they had his feet in place, Murdock plopped down on the passenger's side and Face got back out of the vehicle. Hannibal circled around and raised B.A.'s left arm long enough to change the date on the black man's watch.

'It's the eighth today.' Hannibal thought aloud, adjusting his own timepiece. 'So three days makes it the eleventh. Now all we have to do is keep him away from newspapers, radios, and television sets for a few days and he won't be the wiser.'

'Why do I feel this sinking feeling of doubt?' Face wondered as he rigged his watch.

Hannibal flicked some stray ash from his cigar, then removed a small bottle of smelling salts from his coat and handed it to Murdock, telling him, 'Okay, Murdock. Earn yourself an Oscar and honk us once he's awake'

'Sure thing, Colonel,' Murdock said, letting his Polaroid dangle as he snapped a salute and took the smelling salts. He waited until Hannibal and Face had headed up the front walk and disappeared inside the hotel, then unscrewed the cap and waved the heady vapours under B.A.'s nose.

'. . .'nuther brew, mamma,' B.A. sputtered, surfacing from the epic dream he'd been floating through since going under the gas hours ago. It took a few good whiffs of the salts to wrench him fully to the world of the waking. Bolting upright in the driver's seat, he blinked his eyes with confusion squinting against the sunlight slanting through the windshield. 'Huhhh? What the. . . where am I, man?'

'Wake up! Wake up, B.A.!' Murdock cried out, giving his companion a prod in the shoulder.

'I am awake, fool!' B.A. snapped groggily, blinking the last of his deep sleep from his eyes. Once he was able to focus, he saw the glitter of light playing off the waves of the Atlantic behind the hotel. 'Hey, what are we doin' in Malibu, man?'

'Oh, what a kidder!' Murdock laughed. 'Malibu! Ha, that's rich, B.A.!'

'I don't see what's so funny, sucker,' B.A. groused. 'What's goin' on? Last thing I knew I was gonna get my mouth fixed up by some kiddie dentist!'

'Come off it, B.A., that's ancient history and you know it!' Murdock leaned over and bopped the horn. 'This is Miami Beach, *muchacho*! Just take a look out there, will ya? It's gorgeous! *Magnifique*! Like, cool, Daddio!'

As Murdock started snapping more pictures with his unloaded camera, B.A. scratched his Mandinka, trying to make sense of it all. 'What am I doin' behind the wheel of this heap? Where's my van, man?'

'Look, big guy, I didn't know you were this bad off,' Murdock said. 'I mean, when you pulled to a stop here after driving two days straight and just conked out, I thought you were just exhausted. Sounds to me like there's still some grey matter holding out on you, B.A. . . some of them memory cells, from the sounds of it.'

"I don't remember drivin' for no two days straight!' B.A. insisted.

'Hey, I tried to pitch in, but you wouldn't hear it. No, sir. Don't tell me you can't even remember that big stink we had at the rental place in Tucumcari?' Murdock clucked his tongue at the supposed memory. 'We left the van there 'cause the timing chain gave out, and you bet me two bits that you could still drive anything on four wheels all the way to Miami without fallin' asleep.'

'I did?'

Murdock slipped a quarter in B.A.'s shirt pocket. 'It'll all come back once you've had some real shuteye in the hotel. If you're lucky, they might even have those magic fingers that jiggle the mattress for ya, huh? Heck, you got the quarter already. All you gotta do is feed it into the gizmo and lay back and. . .oh, hey, look! There's the Colonel and Face!'

Hannibal was the first to reach the wagon, shaking his head with mock amazement as he glanced at his watch. 'That sure was fast, guys,' he told B.A. and Murdock. 'We weren't expecting you until later tonight.'

Murdock popped out of the car and pumped Hannibal's hand as if he were greeting a long-lost friend. 'Oh, we had a fine drive, sir. Fine indeed. B.A. here pushed that pedal to the metal like a seasoned pro. Yessir, he was truly amazing.'

'How ya doin', B.A.?' Face asked as Baracus slowly crawled out from behind the steering wheel and began rubbing his stiff back.

'Lousy,' B.A. replied. 'Somethin' funny's goin' on here, and I don't think I like it!'

Murdock reached into his shirt pocket and pulled out nothing but air, although he carried on as if he were holding a handful of snapshots. 'I took some great pics, Colonel. Check it out.' He moved close to Hannibal and pantomimed as he continued, 'Here's a picture of when we drove past the Rio Grande.'

'Uh, Murdock. . .'

'Okay, okay, so it's a little underexposed,' Murdock confessed, quickly flipping to the next invisible shot. 'Now, this one turned out nice, you gotta admit. This is New Mexico. The Indian lady there was selling blankets. I would have bought one, but they didn't look like they'd hold up well on the beach, what with all the sand and rough-housing. They were more like the kind of arty blankets you hang on the wall and look at, know what I mean?'

His curiosity aroused, B.A. moved past Face and looked over Murdock's shoulder. 'Hey, I don't see no pictures!' He started shaking Murdock. 'What gives?'

'Hey, easy, B.A.,' Hannibal intervened, stepping between Murdock and his antagoniser.

'Yeah, big guy,' Murdock said. 'I'm talking interpretation here. A picture, after all, is not merely light sensitive silver nitrate on paper. No sir! A picture is an expression of a feeling! A thought concept of a mood or desire. Don't you understand?'

'The day I understand you I'll be ready for the nut bin, too,' B.A. said.

'Say cheese!' Murdock whipped his Polaroid up in front of his face and snapped a non-picture of B.A.'s snarling countenance. 'Oh, that was great. Wonderful. Just like that portrait shot of Churchill when Karsch took away his cigar. I can't wait to see how it turns out!'

Face loaded the last of the remaining luggage onto a hand cart and jockeyed it up onto the sidewalk, then told the others, 'Look, instead of standing around out here gabbing away, why don't we get B.A. and Murdock checked in so we can all enjoy a little happy hour refreshment?'

'Good idea,' Hannibal agreed.

'I still don't remember drivin' for two days,' B.A. said. As the last effects of the knockout gas wore off, he suddenly became aware of the persistent pain still residing in his mouth. 'Oowwwww. . .and what about this? I thought once that tooth got pulled it wouldn't hurt any more.'

Thinking fast, Face explained, 'The doc said you should expect it to feel like that for a little while. . .how did he describe it?'

'Phantom pains,' Murdock adlibbed. 'Kinda like that Kirlian aura. You know, like when they take a picture of a tree after it sheds a leaf and you can see the energy field still hanging out where the leaf used to be. . .?'

'Shut up, Murdock!' B.A. growled. 'Man, I probably blanked out the past couple of days just because you drove me nuts all the way out here and I didn't want to remember.'

'Hmmmm,' Hannibal speculated, 'That might be the explanation right there.'

'Of course!' Murdock exclaimed. 'Retrograde amnesia! Wherein the patient's power of recall excludes certain traumatic experiences and all events that—'

'Murdock!' Hannibal cut in. 'Save the lecture for another time, okay?'

B.A. suggested, 'I got a better idea. Why don't we ship this sucker back to Hollywood and put him on some game show? With all his goofball knowledge, he could win a bundle and we'd have him out of our hair!'

As the Team continued up the walk, Murdock began sulking and fidgeting with his camera equipment. Hannibal noticed two men approaching Sandy and Tina, who were standing just outside the entrance to the hotel, putting the finishing touches on a hand-painted sign that read: 'OPEN UNDER NEW OWNERSHIP!! TRY OUR NEW INTRODUCTORY RATES!!'

'Okay, gang,' Hannibal told the rest of the team. 'Enough with the intramural squabbles. I think we're about ready to start earning our slice of the action.'

It was Rocky and Eddie, Joey Epic's prize enforcers, who were bearing down on the Conlon sisters. Eddie picked at his bicuspids with a toothpick while Rocky rolled his sleeves up over his biceps. When they reached the hotel entrance, Rocky tapped Sandy on the shoulder and cleared his throat to get her attention.

'You want cough drops, try the drugstore down the street,' Sandy told Rocky.

'I thought we told you how dangerous it might be for you two ladies to keep this place open.'

'There's not much we can do about it,' Sandy replied smugly, pointing to the sign. 'It's not our place any more.'

'I don't get it,' Rocky said. 'What new ownership? Joey didn't tell us nothin' about gettin' the papers to this place yet.'

'That's because he didn't get them,' Tina sneered. 'The new owners are right behind you.'

Rocky and Eddie turned around and saw The A-Team headed their way. They stood side by side, forming a human barricade before the hotel entrance, and waited. When Hannibal reached them, he smiled affably and nodded a greeting. ''lo, gents.'

'We heard a rumour you guys are runnin' this dump now,' Rocky said. 'That true?'

Hannibal reached into his pocket for a slip of paper, then checked the handwriting on it against the hotel marquee. 'Surfsider Hotel. Yep, this is my new baby. Now, if you'll kindly step aside, I'd kinda like to have a look around. . .'

Neither of the behemoth human bookends budged. Eddie advised Hannibal, 'We can spare you the trouble, pal. This place is a bad investment. Things get broken easily. Customers get hit for no reason. There's a bad element around this neighbourhood. . .'

'You boys look like you'd know all about something like that,' Hannibal told the thugs. 'Well, maybe you can help spread the word for me. I'm cleaning up things around here, and anybody that gives me a hard time is gonna end up looking like something our chef sprinkles on pizza.'

'We'll see about that,' Rocky guffawed.

Rocky and Eddie were both wearing shoulder holsters beneath their summer blazers, and as they reached for their guns Murdock beat them to the trigger, activating his portable flash and temporarily blinding the gunmen before they could get off any shots. Hannibal followed up with a rugged right cross that sent Eddie teetering backwards into the sign.

Rocky lunged toward Hannibal while his back was turned, but Face gave the luggage cart a quick shove and clipped the hulk at the shins, toppling him like a fullback being broadsided by a defensive blitz.

'Get inside!' Hannibal told Sandy and Tina seconds before he dived to the pavement, avoiding a stream of bullets pumped his way by Eddie, who had come up firing from behind the sign.

Murdock unslung one of his cameras and swung it around his head by its strap, like a cowboy's lariat. When he let go of the Polaroid, it hurtled through the air and slammed noisily into the sign, distracting Eddie long enough to give Hannibal time to get back on his feet. Snatching up one of the fallen suitcases, Hannibal charged Eddie and batted him to the ground with a convincing swipe of the Samsonite.

'I used to be a bellhop in my youth,' Hannibal told Eddie, who curled up on the sidewalk, groaning with pain. 'I have a way with luggage. . . but, then, how could you have known?'

Rocky had lost his gun and, when he saw that he was outnumbered, he tried to make a run for it, bolting over a knee-high hedge and breaking into a run. Unfortunately for him, however, B.A. was inspired by the chance to take out his pent-up anger on someone besides his team-mates, and with a few long strides, he caught up with the fleeing heavy and grabbed him by the collar of his blazer. 'Where you think you're going', jack?' B.A. shouted, taking hold of the man's belt with his other hand. In a breathtaking display of raw strength, B.A. lifted Rocky up and swung him like a sack of feed into the shallow fountain gushing spouts of water in front of the hotel.

Rocky flailed helplessly in the shallow water, wild with fear. By the time B.A. strode over and yanked him back out, Face and Hannibal were escorting Eddie out to the curb while Murdock flagged down a passing taxi. Before dumping the beaten thugs into the back seat of the cab, The A-Team relieved the men of their wallets and counted out a thick wad of bills.

'There's enough here to cover for the damages to the patio the other day,' Hannibal said, pocketing all the money save for a twenty dollar bill, which he handed to the cab driver, telling him, 'Take these poor gentlemen to the Sunset and hand 'em over to Joey Epic. He'll be expecting them, although not quite in this condition.'

As he closed the back door on Eddie and Rocky, Face told them, 'Oh, and be sure to tell Joey Baby that the Surfsider sends its regards.'

The A-Team stepped back from the curb as the cab pulled away, with the two goons glaring hatefully out of the rear window at them.

'Well,' Hannibal commented calmly, 'I think we just earned ourselves a nice steak and lobster dinner, eh?'

'I think we just earned ourselves some major trouble,' B.A. said.

'That, too,' Hanniball conceded, 'But then, that's what we're here for, right?'

6

Over supper, The A-Team held a strategy meeting, after which everyone retired to their quarters for the first item on their agenda—a good night's sleep. The night clerk was left with instructions to awaken the Team in the event Joey Epic decided to strike back immediately in retaliation for the drubbing his boys had received during their most recent visit to the Surfsider. The night passed without incident, however, and by the time Hannibal had polished off a room service breakfast the following morning, and suited himself up in an all-white outfit that made him look like a country club retiree, the rest of the Team was already out and about.

Sunshine had cut its way through the coastal haze, and there was already a healthy buzz of activity taking place around the hotel's outdoor pool. Sunbathers basked on chaise longues, giving off the pungent aroma of tanning oil. A few children splashed about in the shallow end of the pool while grownups swam laps in the deeper water. Lured by a quickly-placed ad in that morning's paper, a handful of senior citizens had gathered around the nearby shuffleboard courts, where Tina was giving instructions. Waitresses drifted amidst the activity, wearing tastefully stylish bikinis in place of the Polynesian skirts that had been their uniforms prior to Face's arrival the day before.

Face himself was near the pool, engaged in a discussion with two winsome-looking young ladies in shorts and halter tops. He was wearing swim trunks and his hair was still wet from a quick dip in the pool. As Hannibal strolled over to meet him, Face wrapped up the instructions he was giving to the women.

'Good, good. Okay, now I want you and Sheila to hit the major restaurants. . .see if you can get the parking attendants to help you. Don't be afraid to use a little charm.' Face acknowledged Hannibal with a brief nod as he reached for a stack of flyers on the rattan table next to him. He divided the stack in two and gave one pile to each woman. 'I want every car and every person you come across to get one of these, and be sure to tell everyone about the complimentary drinks we're offering with each check-in at the hotel. Okay, got it?'

As the girls nodded and started off, Sheila reminded him, 'And once we're done you'll be giving me those acting lessons we were talking about, right?'

'Natch,' Face said with a wink.

Once the girls were out of earshot, Hannibal moved up next to Face and raised an eyebrow. 'Acting lessons, Face? I thought this was all business at this stage of the game. . .'

'Ah, yeah. . .' Face started towelling his hair. 'Well, Hannibal, we had to get those flyers out, and it isn't easy to find free help these days. I had to rely on a little of the old hook and crook. Besides, with all the scams we've pulled in our time, I think I'm as qualified to teach acting as anyone.'

'You've got me there,' Hannibal said. 'How are B.A. and Murdock holding up on their end?'

'Like oil and water, as usual,' Face replied, gesturing at the other side of the pool. 'See for yourself.'

Hannibal looked over and saw B.A. perched atop the lifeguard station, wearing a swimsuit and all of his jewellery so that he looked more like a guardian for King Tut than a lifeguard. He was holding a pair of binoculars, which he frequently tilted upwards for a glimpse at the skyline beyond the hotel. Murdock paced nearby, still attired in his tourist togs and snapping pictures of everything that moved.

Face and Hannibal leisurely made their way around the pool, pausing now and then to make the guests feel welcome. When they reached the lifeguard station, Hannibal noticed that B.A. had the binoculars trained on a high-rise building down the street.

'Checking out Joey's place?' Hannibal asked.

B.A. nodded without looking away from the hotel. 'No fire escapes that I can see. . . and the penthouse looks like it's got a chopper pad on the roof and a private elevator.'

'Hmmmm, they probably have top-notch security, too,' Hannibal mused. 'Well, nobody said it was going to be easy.'

Murdock rose on his tiptoes and reached for the binoculars. 'Lemme have a look, B.A. . . .'

'No way, fool!' B.A. retorted, swatting Murdock's hand away. 'Use the zoom lens on one of your cameras!'

'I should have the binocs,' Murdock insisted. 'Face said I was supposed to be the lifeguard, after all.'

'You can't even swim, turkey!' B.A. lowered the binoculars and pointed a finger at Murdock. 'Keep buggin' me and I'll squish you like a mosquito!'

'B.A.,' Face said, tapping a finger against the gold chains clinging to Baracus's neck, 'you'd sink if you jumped in the pool with all that jewellery. Come on, be a sport and let Murdock be the lifeguard. We need you for security.'

'Yeah!' Murdock said, holding his hand out. 'Let me have the spyglass and sit up there!'

'Face is right, B.A.,' Hannibal threw in. 'I want you on the prowl, keeping an eye out for a frontal assault.'

'All right, all right!' B.A. grumbled, climbing down from the elevated post and handing the binoculars over to Murdock. 'I just don't dig walkin' around so much 'cause it makes my mouth hurt more. Man, it still aches something fierce!'

'Phantom pains, remember?' Hannibal said.

'Yeah, I guess, but it sure feels like it hurts worse than the real thing.'

'Patience, B.A.!' Hannibal gave Baracus an encouraging pat on the back. 'Maybe you should go back to using some of that cloves extract for the next few days and see if that helps. We need you at your best, partner. We're counting on you for a full lowdown on Epic's hotel. Number of bodyguards, licence numbers on his limos. . . anything you think we can use.'

'I'll do my best,' B.A. promised, then headed off, dabbing his fingertips against his afflicted jaw.

'Maybe we should have had that tooth taken out for him,' Face remarked, watching B.A. disappear inside the hotel.

'Yeah, too bad it was Dr Kalalau's day off when we brought B.A. in,' Hannibal said. 'I sure wasn't about to play dentist in B.A.'s mouth, no matter how much he was knocked out.'

One of the poolside waitresses came by, holding out a tray with a glass of champagne on it. 'Here you are, boss.'

'Thank you, darling,' Face said, taking the drink. He watched the waitress sashay away from him, smiling appreciatively. 'You know, Hannibal, I think my idea of having the help wear bikinis is really gonna pay off.'

'Maybe, as long as that doesn't go for the bellhops and busboys,' Hannibal cracked.

Sandy and Tina emerged from the hotel, wearing shorts and tank tops. Although they seemed pleased with the upswing in business around the pool, Sandy couldn't help but smile stiffly at the sight of the scantily clad waitresses. 'You really seem to have things cooking here, Mister Peck,' she said sarcastically as she and Tina joined up with Face and Hannibal. 'I'm slightly disappointed, though. . . no wet T-shirt contest?'

'That's scheduled for three o'clock, down at the Lanai,' Face countered matter-of-factly. 'You mean the posters aren't up yet? Honestly, do I have to do everything around here?' He headed off, raising a hand to get the attention of a generously endowed blonde bombshell sunning herself near the edge of the pool. 'Oh, Bambi. . .!'

Sandy sighed as she watched Face go about his business. She told Hannibal, 'I don't imagine it's easy keeping everything going when a lot of his time's taken up with hiring out thirty-eights, twenty-fours, and thirty-sixes.'

'Ladies,' Hannibal told Sandy and Tina, 'this is what you might call a little window dressing. It's all part of the master plan.'

'Window dressing?' Sandy exclaimed.

Her sister chimed in, 'Master plan? Are you serious?'

Hannibal nodded sombrely, eyeing a passing waitress out of the corner of his eye. 'As strange as it seems, he's doing this for you. You have to understand, we need to keep this place hot and hopping, because the odds are that even as we speak, our every move is being watched by your friend Joey. . .'

'I don't believe this!' Joey Epic fumed, stepping away from the telescope posted before the window of his penthouse office. He chewed off the end of his cigar and worked the tobacco to an odious pulp before spitting it out in his wastebasket. 'He had the gall to wave at me!'

Epic's office was an elaborate affair, panelled in rich mahogany and filled with stuffed heads and pictures taken during a number of his wild game hunts over the years. One wall was lined with mounted rifles, ranging from an antique muzzle-loader to a modern A-15. His desk consisted of a thick slab of glass perched on two sets of elephant tusks that curved like well-sculpted legs of ivory. Standing on the other side of the desk were Rocky and Eddie, who both were scarred with cuts and bruises from their encounter with The A-Team the day before. They were shame-faced and they studiously avoided meeting Epic's livid gaze as he lit up his cigar and started smoking it furiously, as if it were a short fuse he couldn't wait to reach the end of.

'This stinks!' Epic railed. 'I send you two out there to close that hotel down once and for all and you end up coming back to me lookin' like a pair of used punching bags. And now I take a peek down there and what do I see? I see a booming business down there, that's what I see! The place is crawling with sweet young things parading around in their underwear and enough happy tourists to put the place back in the black by the end of the week!'

'Sorry,' Rocky lamely apologised.

'Oh, that's great!' Epic sneered. 'All is forgiven! Sheeeesh!' He went back to the telescope and planted one eye against the viewer. 'He's *still* waving at me, the smug little jerk! Rubbing it in!'

'If you want, Mr Epic, we can—'

'Hey, you're bleeding on my carpet, you cretin!' Epic roared, pointing at Eddie's lip.

As he brought out a handkerchief and pressed it against the cut, Eddie tried to explain, 'Mr Epic, those guys were professionals. I mean, we're not talking about a couple of beach boys the girls found hanging out by the pool. They knew what they was doing. . .'

'What they *were* doing!' Epic corrected. 'Look, if you can't do anything else right, you can at least watch your grammar!'

'Eddie's right, though,' Rocky said. 'About the guys who took over down there, that is. They're tough, and if we're gonna take 'em out, it's gonna take more than the two of us.'

'Shut up!' Joey exploded, throwing his cigar at Rocky. He missed, and the cigar bounded off the nose of a moose head before tumbling onto the carpet. Eddie quickly snatched it up and handed it back to Joey, who jammed it back in his mouth without bothering to light it back up. As he stalked back and forth, he continued laying into his cohorts. 'Do you think I look like dog food here? Look, I don't need excuses, and I don't want 'em, either, got that? What I need. . .what I *want* is the deed to that hotel, and I want it by the end of the week. If I don't have it by the end of the week, we're all gonna be slapped in cellophane and shipped to a butcher shop as hamburger patties. Am I making myself clear?'

'Yeah, Mr Epic,' Eddie uttered meekly.

'What did you say?'

Eddie stiffened and raised his voice. 'Yes, sir, Mr Epic!'

'Good!' Epic said. 'I want that hotel!'

'We'll do all we can, sir,' Rocky promised, 'but those guys down there aren't going to just give it to us.'

'Now, that's very brilliant on your part, Einstein,' Epic told Rocky. He reached across his desk for a small derringer and aimed it at his associates, then pulled the trigger. A tongue of flame flickered out from the tip of the barrel, and Epic tilted it up to relight his cigar. Blowing smoke in Rocky's face, he said, 'Maybe they won't give the hotel to us, but that doesn't mean we can't take it.'

Rocky stifled a cough. 'Sir? I don't understand.'

'I wouldn't expect you to.' Joey went back to the telescope. Before peering into it, he glanced back at Eddie and Rocky. 'Now get outta here until I need you again. I'm gonna handle our next move on my own.'

After the two thugs shuffled out of the office, Joey went back to spying on the Surfsider Hotel, letting his new plan formulate itself in his mind. A few minutes later, he was startled by the buzz of his intercom.

'Now what?' Epic grumbled, moving over to the desk and pressing the 'talk' button. 'Yes, Shirley?'

'Long distance call for you, Mr Epic,' came the tiny voice of Joey's secretary over the intercom speaker. 'From Chicago. A Mr Carlin. Will you take the call?'

At the mention of Carlin's name, Epic began to tremble. He choked on his own cigar smoke and began to gag.

'Excuse me, Mr Epic, I didn't catch that? Do you want to take this call?'

'No!' Epic sputtered. 'Tell him I'm out!'

'He said it was urgent!'

'Damn it, tell him I'm not in and take a message! Do you understand?'

'Yes, sir.'

As he let go of the intercom button and slumped into his chair, Epic began to sweat. Time was running out for him. 'That hotel,' he muttered, nearly delirious. 'I gotta have that hotel!'

8

There was a fast food stand that serviced the pool area of the Surfsider, offering a limited menu of hamburgers, hot dogs, fries, and soft drinks. Business was brisk, and both Face and Hannibal were supervising as a pair of teenage girls tried to keep up with the steady demand of patrons lined up before the stand.

'Whoah, whoah,' Face gasped, waving his arms like a referee signalling a foul. He moved over to where one of the girls was applying condiments to a hamburger. 'Easy on the mustard, sweetheart.'

'Oh, sorry, Mr Peck,' the girl said, moving away to let Face step in and show her his idea of the proper technique.

'One spot of mustard,' he said, giving the shaker bottle a slight squeeze. 'Then a couple of pickles. . .two, to be exact, placed just so. . .'

Hannibal smiled wryly and told Face, 'You're quite the *artiste*, there, "Mr Peck". Tell me, how'd you master such finesse?'

'I was head cook at the orphanage for a of couple years,' Face divulged modestly. 'I hate to brag, but in my prime I could handle a spatula the way Picasso handled a paintbrush.'

'That's good to know,' Hannibal said, spotting someone

of interest out in the crowd gathered around the pool. 'Since you're such an expert, I'll leave you to the coaching here and go mingle among the patrons.'

'Suit yourself.' Face grabbed a hot dog bun and reached into a steam cooker with a set of tongs, telling the girl next to him, 'Now, let's move along to the tube steak. . .'

'Don't you mean the weiner?' the girl asked with a giggle. The other teenager blushed and looked the other way.

'Tell you what,' Face said, withdrawing a frank and slipping it into the bun. 'Let's just call 'em hot dogs, okay?'

As Hannibal wove his way through the poolside throng, he halfheartedly greeted anyone he made eye contact with, but his primary attention was focused on a long-legged redhead who looked like this year's winner in the Miss Universe swimsuit competition. She filled out a tight bikini the way a crack accountant filled out an income tax form. As it turned out, the woman was seeking out Hannibal, and when they finally reached one another, she held out a room key for him to see.

'Excuse me, but aren't you the owner?' she asked.

'I sure am,' Hannibal admitted. 'How can I help you?'

'It's this key,' she said with exasperation. 'I've tried and tried, but I just can't seem to make it fit in the lock to my room. I was wondering if maybe, well. . .'

Hannibal reached out and took the key. 'I'll be glad to give it a try. I'm very good at locks. As a matter of fact, in my prime, I could handle a key the way Picasso handled a paintbrush.'

The woman laughed, 'What a delightful sense of humour you have!'

'Aw, gee,' Hannibal drawled, 'these things just pop right out without me thinking about 'em. It's no big thing.'

As they left the crowd behind and headed down the back walkway leading to the rear of the hotel, the woman said, 'I really appreciate you taking the time to do this for me. I was looking for a bellboy but couldn't seem to find one, so I—'

'Please,' Hannibal interrupted, 'it's my pleasure, believe me. Here at the Surfsider we pride ourselves in the personal touch. By the way, my name is Smith. Hannibal Smith.'

'Denise,' the woman said, smiling coquettishly. 'Tell me, just how personal is this touch of yours?'

'Well, let's just say that satisfaction is guaranteed. . .'

'Ohhhhh, my my my,' Denise purred, reaching into her purse. 'I guess you must have received a pretty high rating, hmmmm?'

'Four stars all the way!'

When Denise removed her hand from her purse, it was attached to a gun, and its business end was pointing at Hannibal. Suddenly cold, she warned Hannibal, 'One wrong move and you'll be number one with a bullet.'

Hannibal put his hands in the air without an invitation. 'And what a fine sense of humour *you* have. I don't suppose that might be a squirt gun by any chance.'

Denise pulled back the hammer. 'Hardly.'

'I didn't think so.'

'I changed my mind about the lock,' Denise said, taking the key back from Hannibal.

'Funny, so did I.'

'Okay, now I want you to drop your arms and walk in front of me to the parking lot, Mr Smith. We don't want to arouse anyone's suspicions, now, do we?'

Unbeknownst to Denise, suspicions had already been aroused, in the person of Howling Mad Murdock, who was watching Hannibal's abduction through binoculars from his elevated perch on the lifeguard stand. Face and B.A. had come over to join him.

'She one of Joey's?' Face asked Murdock.

'Yup,' Murdock said, panning with the binoculars to keep Denise and Hannibal in the sights. 'Hannibal was right on the money when he figured they'd try to fight bikinis with bikinis. Mamma mia, she came off the line with all the optional equipment, believe me. . .'

'Gimme that!' B.A. snapped, climbing up the first few

rungs of the ladder and swiping the binoculars from Murdock. Once he picked up Denise and Hannibal, he murmured, 'Man, I sure hope she doesn't plan to torture him.'

'Okay, let's not be hogs here,' Face said, making his play for the binoculars.

'Hey, hey,' Murdock said, bringing his lifeguard whistle to his lips and threatening to blow it. 'It's against pool regulations to crowd the lifeguard.'

'Shut up, fool!' B.A. yelled while Face kept staring through the binoculars until Denise and Hannibal had moved out of view.

'Well, he's on his own now,' Face said, 'I sure hope this Trojan Horse plan of his works.'

'Don't worry, man,' B.A. said, 'They won't have him to themselves for all that long. Come on, let's get ready to move out. . .'

As Denise prodded Hannibal to keep walking before her, Eddie and Rocky suddenly jumped out from behind the hedges growing alongside the hotel. Their guns were bigger than Denise's so she put hers away.

'We meet again,' Rocky told Hannibal.

'I hate corny clichés,' Hannibal complained, stifling a yawn.

'Well, I got another good one for you,' Rocky said, 'How about "One false move and you're dead"?'

'Good. Good, I like that,' Hannibal confessed. 'Only what's the difference between a false move and a true one?'

Rocky grabbed Hannibal by the arm and turned him around. 'Now why don't you head over to that black limo parked over there? And here's another one. . ."Don't try anything funny"!'

Both Rocky and Eddie laughed at Rocky's wit, but Hannibal glanced at Denise and wisecracked, 'He should have quit while he was ahead. You're much better with the jokes.'

As she walked alongside Hannibal, Denise told him,

'I'm disappointed with you, Mister Smith. You made it very easy for us.'

'What can I say?' Hannibal shrugged his shoulders. 'Listen, would you mind if I smoked?'

As Hannibal reached for one of his cigars, Eddie whirled around and aimed his gun at Hannibal's heart. 'Freeze!' he shouted.

'Hey, take it easy,' Hannibal said, producing the cigar. 'Don't worry, it's not loaded. And why don't you point that popgun somewhere else? Somebody could get hurt, and Mr Epic wouldn't like that. I'm sure he wants me in one piece. . .'

9

Joey Epic was feeling back on top of things by the time Hannibal was brought into his office. Eighteen holes of golf and three martinis at the clubhouse bar had done wonders at relieving his anxieties, and the news that his use of Denise to apprehend the new owner of the Surfsider Hotel had been effective was enough to make his day.

'Well, hello there, Mr Smith,' Epic greeted Hannibal as he motioned to an overstuffed chair near his desk. 'So nice of you to drop by.'

'You sent out such a charming welcome wagon, I could hardly resist,' Hannibal said as he slipped into the chair and looked around at the trophy heads mounted on the walls. 'Nice collection, Joey, but I thought I'd see a few humans up there, you being such a corporate head-hunter and all.'

'You misjudge me,' Epic insisted. 'When it comes to business, I have no need for a killer instinct. I just provide people with certain opportunities and give them a chance to see the wisdom in what I'm offering. As a matter of fact, I have just such an offer for you.'

Epic pulled a few papers from a manilla folder and handed them to Hannibal. As he started reading over the document, Hannibal told Epic, 'I can usually read contracts better with a good cigar. From the smell of it, I'd say you have a nice stash of Havanas around here somewhere. . .'

Joey snapped his fingers. Rocky moved away from the doorway, which he was guarding with Eddie, and retrieved a cigar from the humidor at the far corner of Epic's desk. Hannibal took it and clamped it between his jaws, then waited patiently for Rocky to light it. Rocky looked to his boss, who nodded his head. Making a face, Rocky took a lighter from his pocket and coaxed a flame from it. After Hannibal puffed the cigar to life, he blew smoke into Rocky's face. 'Thanks, pal. You can go crawl back into the woodwork now.'

As he put his lighter away, Rocky muttered under his breath, 'Keep askin' for it and you'll get it.'

'That's a pretty good one, too,' Hannibal said, 'Only the way I've always heard it, it goes "Ask and ye shall receive".'

Rocky's face flushed an interesting shade of crimson, but a warning glance from Joey prevented him from acting on his temper. The thug returned to his post while Hannibal finished skimming through the contract, which dealt with the transferral of ownership of the Surfsider Hotel to Joey Epic for a sum less than half its market value.

'You sign right on the dotted line,' Epic told Hannibal.

Hannibal set the contract down on the desk and pointed to the line in question. 'Right here?'

'That's all there is to it, then you can turn around and walk out of here in one piece.' Joey grinned. 'It's so much easier to enjoy an early retirement when you have your health.'

Rather than using a pen, Hannibal signed the contract with the burning tip of his cigar, and within seconds the papers were aflame. Joey leaned across the desk and grabbed the blazing document, shaking out the fire, but not before most of the contract was charred beyond recognition.

'Well, I gotta be honest, Joey baby,' Hannibal confessed. 'I read the terms and I don't like 'em. Then, too, there's the fact that I'm not really interested in selling the hotel in the first place.' There was now more than an inch of ash on Hannibal's cigar, and he tapped it off onto Epic's desktop.

'You're a very stupid man,' Joey responded coldly, his good mood gone up in the smoke that still curled up from the scorched contract.

'For someone who's very stupid, I sure know how to run a hotel, eh?' Hannibal glanced over at the telescope by the window. 'I see where you've had a chance to see how much business is booming at the Surfsider since I took over.'

'I'll put it to you one more time, Mr Smith,' Joey said, removing a copy of the contract from his folder and setting it out on the desk. 'Sign the Surfsider over to me and you'll leave here with enough teeth in your head to hold onto that cigar.'

'Tell you what, Joey, how about we trade even up, the Sunset for the Surfsider? Now there's a deal I might think about.'

Joey sighed and gestured over Hannibal's shoulder to Rocky and Eddie, telling them, 'Boys, I'm afraid we're going to have to submit Mr Smith to binding arbitration.'

'Gladly,' Rocky said as he and Eddie came up behind Hannibal. Eddie plucked the cigar from Hannibal's mouth and Rocky pinned The A-Team leader's arms behind his back. After he put the cigar out, Eddie closed his right hand into a fist and slammed it into Hannibal's stomach, doubling him over.

'That's to pay you back for yesterday,' Eddie said. 'This one's interest.'

As Hannibal took a second blow to the midsection, Joey told him, 'There's one thing you have to understand, Mr Smith. I'm gonna get that hotel, even if it has to be over your dead body. Now, you can be smart and take my terms. . . or you can go on being stupid and end up playing volleyball with the sand crabs.'

The wind had been knocked out of Hannibal, and it took him several seconds to get it back. He kept up a confident grin all the while, and once he was able to speak, he cracked, 'I was never any good at volleyball. Those net shots always tripped me up.'

'Gallows humour. How charming.' Joey reached to the humidor and helped himself to one of the cigars. 'I take it that your answer is still no, Mr Smith?'

'Joey, you and I both know I gotta have that hotel. When it comes to business deals, I'm sharp as a tack.' Hannibal turned his head and winked at Rocky. 'Another corny cliché, eh?'

It seemed like nothing more than another display of defiant bravado, but something Hannibal said caught Joey off guard. 'What are you talking about?' he demanded angrily.

Hannibal saw Epic's fingers trembling around his cigar and realised he'd struck a nerve. 'Oh, yeah. . .play dumb with me, Joey,' he said, milking his bluff. 'C'mon, do you think I would have taken over a dying hotel if I didn't know *why* you had to have it?'

'Don't play games with me, Smith.'

Hannibal ignored Epic's taunt and smirked at Rocky again. 'Sharp as a tack, remember?'

'You don't know nothin',' Epic said, without much conviction.

'I wouldn't bet on that if I were you, chump.'

Epic snapped the cigar between his fingers and told Hannibal, 'You just signed your death warrant!'

'And you just wasted a fine cigar,' Hannibal said.

Epic screamed at his goons, 'Waste *him*!'

Eddie and Rocky sandwiched Hannibal between him and spirited him out of the office, leaving Joey alone with his growing fear. For several moments, he paced in front of his desk, trying to decide on his next course of action. He finally grabbed the phone and punched out a series of numbers. He got an answer on the fifth ring and said, 'I'd like to speak to Councilman Bonitelli. . .'

10

As Rocky and Eddie held Hannibal and waited for the private elevator, Denise emerged from a room down the hall and walked over to the men.

'So, how did things come out, Mr Smith?' she asked Hannibal. 'I trust you listened to reason.'

'No, but I listened to your boyfriend,' Hannibal deadpanned. 'He's a funny man. Puts me in stitches.'

'Stitches won't help when we're done with you, hotshot,' Eddie promised.

Denise's glib smile softened. She eyed Joey's thugs and asked, 'You aren't going to hurt him, are you?'

'Naw,' Rocky joshed, 'If he behaves himself, it'll be over so quick he won't feel a thing.'

'But, I thought—'

'What's the matter, sweetheart,' Hannibal interrupted her, 'didn't you think Joey was gonna be playing for keeps when you turned me over to him?'

Denise seemed genuinely worried now. 'I didn't think you'd have to be hurt. I figured you'd take Joey's offer and it'd be done with. I mean, everyone's supposed to have their price.'

'That sounds like something I'd expect to hear out of Rocky,' Hannibal said. Just then the elevator doors swung open and Hannibal was roughly dragged inside. Before the doors hissed shut, he looked back at Denise and said, 'I'm on your conscience, doll. You better catch up on your sleep while you can, 'cause I'm sure I'll come back as the kind of ghost who'll haunt you the rest of your days.'

The closing doors blocked Denise from Hannibal's view before he could gauge her reaction. As they began to descend to the ground floor, Eddie indulged himself by planting his elbow sharply into Hannibal's side. 'What's the big idea of tryin' to scare her?'

Hannibal shrugged, 'I dunno. Just a whim, I guess. Look at it this way, I could have asked her out for my last meal and won her over with my charm. Then where would she be?'

'Your last meal's gonna be whatever bugs you can eat in the swamp before the gators get to you,' Eddie said.

The elevator slowed to a stop and the three men stepped out into the lobby. As Rocky nudged Hannibal along, he chortled, 'Guess that's gonna make you Gator Aid, huh? Get it? Aid for—'

'Yeah, I get it, Rock 'ol boy,' Hannibal drawled. 'I tell ya what, though, if you really want to get rid of me in a way that'll hurt, forget the alligators and just put me in a dark room and tell me jokes for a few hours straight.'

Two more hulking figures rose from chairs in the lobby and headed over to join Hannibal's escort. Rocky told Hannibal, 'This here's Jim and Kingsley. They'll be taking you for a ride to the swamp. Kingsley's good with a machete. When he's done with you, you'll think you just went through a Veg-o-Matic.'

'Hi, guys!' Hannibal said cheerily. 'Listen, Rocky here already tells me I can't have a last meal, but do you think I could maybe toke on a cigar on the way to the swamp? I've got some in my pocket. I'd get one myself but I have these two growths on my arms that make it kinda hard for me to move.'

Jim, who was the largest Cuban Hannibal had ever laid eyes on, grunted and reached into the pocket of Hannibal's coat. Just as he was about to withdraw a cigar, a loud and sudden explosion ripped through the lobby.

With a shower of twisting metal and shattered glass, a thick-bumpered van barrelled through the front entrance to the hotel and fishtailed to a dramatic halt in the middle of the ground floor.

'What the—'

Jim's words were cut short as Hannibal butted him in the face with the top of his head. The Cuban staggered back into Kingsley, a British heavy with a thick handlebar moustache. While the two men became tangled in each other's flailing limbs, Rocky and Eddie turned their attention to the van, which had 'SURFSIDER HOTEL' emblazoned on its sides. The rear doors of the vehicle swung open like vertical jaws, and both Murdock and Face leaned out, spraying the lobby with rounds from their A-15s. B.A. rolled down his window and fired a .45 from behind the wheel, adding further to the commotion.

As Rocky and Eddie ducked for cover and yanked out their handguns, Hannibal broke into a run, sidestepping Jim and Kingsley.

'Hannibal, catch!' Murdock shouted, tossing a Mac-10 from the back of the van.

Hannibal caught the weapon and spun around, eating holes in the sofa Rocky was hiding behind. Pinned by the gunfire, Rocky was unable to return fire. The rest of The A-Team continued to hold the others at bay with a steady stream of bullets that depreciated the lobby at the rate of roughly a thousand dollars a second. Epic's besieged mob relented under the assault and, to a man, they threw up their hands in surrender.

'Toss your guns out where we can see them!' Hannibal ordered as the sound of gunfire ceased.

One by one, the lobby carpet became dotted with pistols, and the disarmed men moved away from their cover. Eddie, however, hung back out of sight behind the bell captain's desk, a .38 still clenched in his fist. He waited until Kingsley had moved in front of him, giving him enough cover to break out into the open. Before he could take The A-Team by surprise, however, he found the carpeting at his feet being chewed up by a burst from B.A.'s gun.

'Don't move, sucker!' B.A. advised.

Hannibal moved over and relieved Eddie of his revolver, then waved to a cowering young man near the registration desk. 'We've looked the place over and decided we're not gonna check in. It's too messy for our tastes, I'm afraid.'

The A-Team slowly retreated back into the van, then B.A. revved the engine and churned up a spray of carpet nap as the van sped back out through the mangled opening it had created making its grand entrance.

11

'My lobby!' Joey gasped the moment he stepped out of the elevator and viewed the carnage. 'Look what they did to my lobby!'

'They had heavy artillery, boss,' Rocky said. 'Once they crashed through and put the drop on us, there wasn't much we could do. Jim and Kingsley ran out and tried chasin' 'em in one of the limos, but they were already long gone. These guys are commandoes, I'm tellin' ya!'

'Yeah, and you guys are a pack of yellow-bellied cowards!' Joey kicked a bullet-riddled ashtray halfway across the lobby, sending sand and cigarette butts flying. He eyed his small army of jabrones and spat in their general vicinity. 'What do I pay you for? Huh?'

Nobody spoke. Most of the behemoths started to stare at their Florsheims, burning with shame and rage at the indignity they'd suffered. A brooding silence filled the room as Joey slowly walked over to the entrance and stared at the collapsed doorway. His own anger was now beyond words, and his knuckles turned white as he squeezed his hands together.

The ringing of the desk phone clanged through the quiet, startling more than one of the men. The desk clerk stepped around a heap of rubble and spoke briefly into the phone, then cupped his hand over the mouthpiece and called out to Epic, 'It's Mr Carlin from Chicago. He insists on talking to you.'

Epic's face turned the colour of his knuckles and he looked upon the devastated lobby with even more horror. He shook his head frantically as he crossed the room in long strides, then hissed at the desk clerk, 'I'm still not back. Tell him I was called away for the rest of the day on business.'

The clerk passed along the message, and from the changing expression on his face, it was clear that Epic's excuse wasn't holding much sway with the man on the other end of the line. Covering the mouthpiece again, the clerk told Joey, 'He says that if he doesn't talk to you personally within the next five minutes, he's going to book a jet out of Chicago and pay a visit here with the Cardenac brothers.'

Epic's insides were beginning to feel like the lobby looked. He tried not to let his men see his fear, but it oozed out of him in a steady flow of cold sweat. 'Tell him that you'll page me and I'll get back to him right away. I'm going up to my office.'

On his way to the elevators, Epic told Rocky, 'Get this mess cleaned up, then I want everybody to report to me in the upstairs conference room. That's everybody. No days off and everybody pulls double-time until we get things back to working order!'

It was only when he was alone inside the rising elevator that Epic could loosen the reins of his emotion, and as he trembled from head to toe, he let out an exhalation that was part whimper. In his mind's eye, he could picture Mr Carlin, fat and demonic behind a pair of owlish spectacles, making the phone calls from a luxurious office overlooking the Chicago loop. Carlin, Epic's long-time mentor and, as Carlin himself liked to quip, his long-time tormentor as well, had been a high-ranking figure in the Chicago mob for almost half a century. In the world of organised crime, it wasn't easy for anyone to keep their hand in the pie for so many years, but Carlin wasn't just anyone. His power base was supported by an army of hit men rivalling that of the CIA and KGB combined. The Cardenac brothers were his prime enforcers, a pair of cold-hearted killers who were acknowledged masters of at least two dozen different styles of execution and always eager to try out something new and more fiendishly clever. For Epic to think he could stand up to Carlin and the Cardenacs was like the Musketeers thinking they could take on the Marines.

Reaching the penthouse, Joey stepped out of the elevator to find Denise in the hallway, waiting to take a ride down.

'Joey! What was all that noise downstairs?' she gasped. 'I was trying to track you down when I heard this—'

'I don't want to talk about it!' Joey cut in as he stalked past her towards his office. 'Just leave me alone for a few minutes, okay?'

'But I wanted to talk to you about Hannibal Smith.'

Joey paused before his door and turned to face Denise. 'What about him?'

'You. . . you weren't really thinking of getting rid of him, were you?'

'What does it matter?' Joey roared. 'He managed to get rid of himself!'

'Oh, no!'

'Oh, yes! That noise downstairs was him making a getaway, right in the lobby of my own hotel!'

'Oh, really?' She tried to sound as if she shared Epic's disappointment, but she was secretly glad to have been spared the chance of having Hannibal's death on her conscience as well as his ghost in her dreams. Joey detected her relief, and he suddenly reached out and grabbed her.

'Hey, do you know something here that I don't know?' he demanded.

'No, no, of course not!' Denise said, trying to unclamp his hands from her arms. 'Stop it, you're hurting me!'

'Maybe you like this Smith guy and sorta helped his buddies spring him, is that it?'

'No Joey! Honest. Now please, let go of me!'

'Ah, the hell with it!' He pushed Denise away and slipped inside his office, then slammed the door behind him. He knew that he could do only one thing and that was to tell the truth. Any attempt to cover up what had happened would only backfire, because when Carlin wanted to get to the bottom of any matter, he had a way of learning the truth in the time it took him to make a few well-placed phone calls. Joey went to his bar long enough to fortify himself with a double shot of bourbon, then slipped into his chair and put a call through to Chicago on his speaker phone. When he got through to Carlin, he quickly apologised for not getting back to him sooner, then plunged headlong into an explanation as to what had just happened at the hotel. It wasn't pretty, and when there was nothing but silence on the other end after he was finished, Joey knew that honesty wasn't going to score him any points in the face of failure. When Carlin still refused to respond to the news, Joey took a deep breath and tried to shrug the incident off.

'Okay, okay. . .so we had a little trouble. Nothing I can't handle.'

'A little trouble?' Carlin's deep, sonorous voice droned over the speaker phone. There was more menace in his calm than if he had shouted. 'How could you let this happen, Joey?'

'I don't know,' Joey blubbered, mopping his brow with a handkerchief. 'They came through in a van! Crashed right through the main entrance! What were we supposed to do?'

'What could you do? I guess I didn't teach you very much, did I, Joey?' Epic knew he was in for an overly familiar lecture, but he had no choice but to listen to it. There was a sigh on the other end of the line, then Carlin continued, 'My sister used to leave you with me when she went away. I used to rock you on my lap when you were a baby. I watched my sister change your diapers. . .and now I guess *I* gotta change 'em for you, huh, Joey? I don't like that.'

'Listen, Mr Carlin,' Epic bartered, his voice almost squeaking with terror. 'I called a meeting with Mike

Bonitelli tonight. I'm checking out Smith's story. I'll find out if the Councilman's been talking. I tell ya, I'm taking care of everything!'

There was a lingering silence, then Carlin said, 'I'd sure like to believe that, Joey. It would make my day.'

'Then you have my word on it.'

Fair enough, Joey, but I warn you. . .I'm coming down there to check on things soon, and if I don't like what I see, I'm gonna have more than your word. I'll have your head! Take care, Joey. . .'

As he hung up his phone, Joey slowly looked around at the trophy heads hanging from his wall. He reflexively reached for his neck and rubbed it longingly.

12

It wasn't Hannibal Smith's nature to let the enemy know when he was hurt, so it wasn't until he was back at the Surfsider with the rest of the Team that he bothered to mention the fact it felt as if half his ribs had been broken when Joey's goons had used his belly for a punching bag. As the team gathered in the hotel's office to discuss strategy, Sandy insisted that Hannibal take off his shirt so that she could at least tape his ribs, since he'd already insisted that he had too much to do to bother with a trip to the hospital.

'Ohhhhh, easy,' Hannibal grimaced as both sisters collaborated to make sure the tape was bound as tightly around his torso as possible. 'Easy, ladies, please. This tape is supposed to act like a brace, not a tourniquet!'

'Quit your complaining,' Sandy chided. 'You're the one whose idea it was to go and get yourself beat up.'

'I did not get beat up,' Hannibal begged to differ. 'I was running interference on Epic to get him to make his move. . . and I got hit in the process. Trust me, the warranty ran out on me a long time ago, so I'm not about to deliberately put myself through anything that's going to damage any major parts.'

'Bull,' B.A. countered, telling Sandy, 'When Hannibal

gets on the jazz, he'll risk his neck for a good laugh without battin' an eyelash and. . .yeoooow!'

'That tooth still bothering you, B.A.?' Face asked. 'Maybe it's got something to do with all that gunfire we got caught up in. You know, the vibrations and whatnot. . . maybe some nerves keep getting shook up so they're touching each other or something.'

B.A. made another exploratory application of the cloves extract inside his mouth, then wiped his fingers off on a towel as he complained, 'Man, I can't even feel a gap where that bad tooth used to be! Are you sure he didn't just leave it in there?'

The other members of the Team traded glances. Hannibal winked to indicate that he had a cover story, which he proceeded to lay out before B.A. 'You have to realise that one of the reasons the tooth was hurting in the first place was because it was getting crunched between two of your rear molars. Dr. Kalalau said that as soon as he pulled out the bad one, the other two would probably slide over and just sorta fall into place. So, much as it hurts, at least you know that you'll have a straighter smile. That oughta count for something, right?'

'I never smile, so who cares?' B.A. grumbled.

Tina cut the last strip of tape and pressed it in place over Hannibal's lower ribs as she said, 'Now that we've declared war on Joey Epic, I hope that one of you guys has a plan to keep him from stepping on us like we were a bug.'

'Hannibal will come through for us there,' Murdock said enthusiastically. His eyes sparkled like signal lights warning that his ever-unstable psyche was about to dredge up some prime babble. 'Hannibal always has a plan. Why, I'll bet he's formulating one right now.'

'Murdock. . .'

Murdock ignored Face and crept closer to Hannibal, eyeing the other man's head as if it were a crystal ball just coming into focus. 'Oh, yes, his mind is churning, instigating the thought processes. A tiny nucleus of an idea is being postulated in a growing, forming thought that will, in turn, mould itself into a plan! Oh, what a thing of beauty. . . right, Hannibal? You do have a plan, don't you?'

'Yes, but after that fanfare it's apt to be anti-climatic.'
Hannibal rose from the edge of the desk where he'd been
sitting and winced as he tested his mobility with the tape
around his ribs. 'Our friend Joey's got to have a damn
good reason to go after this hotel. When I pretended to
know what it was, he got a bad case of the shakes, so
something heavy duty's got to be coming down. My guess
is that now he'll have to make a move that could end up
tipping his hand. . .provided we can be around when he
makes it.'

The office phone rang and Face snatched it up on the
second ring. ''lo, Surfsider Hotel, the peach by the beach.'
Everyone was looking at him, so he interrupted the
person on the other end of the line long enough to tell the
group that it was just the front desk with a business
problem and had nothing to do with Joey Epic. 'Okay,' he
said back into the mouthpiece once the clerk had laid out
the problem. 'Okay, we got two junkets comin' in at
eleven-thirty. That doesn't have to be a problem if we
make a few minor adjustments. Just make sure to tell 'em
the Sunshine Suites go double the normal rates, but that
we'll throw in a bottle of complimentary champagne along
with the free drinks when they sign in. Got that. . .?
Good, get right on it.'

As soon as Face hung up, Tina said. 'Sunshine Suite?
Mr Peck, we don't have any suites here at all.'

'Hey, all we do is knock out a couple of walls, slap up a
little wallpaper and—poof!—instant suite. Trust me!'
Face turned to Hannibal. 'Okay, where were we? Something about getting the goods on Joey. . .'

'Right,' Hannibal said. 'I think our best bet is his girlfriend, Denise. I sort of primed her the last time I saw her,
and I think she could be the weakest link in Epic's armour.
All we gotta do is find a way to get our hands on her.'

'Ha!' Sandy snickered. 'You're going to have to pick a
number for more convenient service on that count. Half
the men in Miami would like to get their hands on that
woman. It's gotten so bad that when she goes for her daily

skinny-dip she's gotta have bodyguards to keep away the Peeping Toms, Dicks, and Harrys.'

'Oh yeah?' Hannibal said, raising an eyebrow. 'And where does she do her dipping?'

'Beats me,' Sandy said. 'All I know is the gossip, and it's never gotten that specific.'

'Not so, sis,' Tina corrected. 'I remember hearing someone say she uses that private cove just around the bend from Sunset.'

'Excellent!' Hannibal looked over at Face. 'Well, partner. You're the ladies' man around here. This sounds like your assignment.'

'Me! Ladies' Man? No, there must be some mistake.'

'I don't think so, Face.' Hannibal put a hand on Face's shoulder. 'All you have to do is drop by, say hi, then charm a few secrets out of her.'

'Hannibal, Hannibal.' Face took the other man's hand off his shoulder and shook his head. 'Aren't we talking about that sweet, beautiful creature that pulled the .22 on you? The one who carries around two bodyguards so she always has a spare in case one gets a flat? No way, pal. I'd be better off sayin' hello to Colonel Khadaffi in a health spa! This is a mobster's moll and you want me to meet her while she's naked?'

'Yeah, I know it's a dirty job,' Hannibal drawled, reaching to his pocket for a cigar. 'But someone's gotta do it. . .'

13

The morning surf was choppy around the cove, sending wave after wave of white foam rolling ashore with a steady, lulling rhythm. Denise had already gone for her swim, and she had a towel wrapped around her as she skimmed through the morning paper, fighting off a pleasant lethargy that came from the play of the waves and the relaxing rays of the rising sun. A few yards away, two bodyguards basked in small wicker chairs, their searching eyes hidden behind the dark lenses of their sunglasses. Tony was Jim the Cuban's baby brother, which meant that he weighed perhaps a few pounds less, although one would have had trouble noticing. The other bodyguard was a lumbering Swede named Harold, who looked like Ingmar Bergman's answer to Arnold Schwarzenegger.

Above the pounding of the surf, a handful of gulls played in the air, shrieking happily as they rode the breeze. Then a more human, less joyful cry sounded from the waters.

'Help! Help me, I'm drowning!'

It was Templeton Peck, three-time freestyle swimming champion at St Bartholomew's Orphanage, floundering in the surf and thrashing his arms like someone trying unsuccessfully to apply the principles of karate to the art of the breaststroke.

'Help!' he spluttered again, glancing through the frenzied mist he was whipping up. When he was sure he had Denise's attention, he cried out, 'I'm going under!', and then promptly did so, slipping beneath the chilled waters.

'My gosh, he needs help!' Denise shouted, bolting to her feet and casting off her towel. Contrary to the local gossip, she wasn't naked, although her string bikini left precious little to the imagination. As she charged to the surf, she called back to her bodyguards, 'Get something! Something that floats!'

Face resurfaced momentarily, filling his lungs with fresh air as he flailed his arms with supposed helplessness. When he saw Denise run into the water and then dive headlong towards him, he held his breath and went down for the second time. Within moments he felt smooth hands reaching for him, bearing him up from the depths. Denise secured a trained lifeguard's hold on Face, cradling one arm around his neck and using the other to swim back toward shore. Face himself had rescued enough sinking swimmers to know how victims tended to react, and he put on a creditable performance, spluttering loudly and continuing to slap the waves with his arms.

'Thank God!' he gasped between breaths. 'Thank God!'

'Quiet!' Denise told him. 'And stop moving so much! You'll be all right if you relax and let me get you to land.'

Face complied with the request, although he had to fight back his apprehension as the two bodyguards waded into the ocean to help retrieve him. It was only when he was close enough to see them clearly that Face was able to assure himself that neither of the men had been in the lobby of the Sunset Hotel the day before, when he'd helped B.A. and Murdock rescue Hannibal from his impending execution. Harold tossed aside the boogie board he'd carried into the surf and grabbed Face by the armpits, dragging him the rest of the way ashore and setting him down on the white sand. When Denise crouched over beside him, concern in her eyes, Face pulled out all the stops.

'I was goin',' he muttered weakly as he gulped for air. 'I was goin' real fast. My whole life was passing before my eyes. I saw my little red bike. And my GI Joe doll. Sister Margaret at the orphanage, putting a star by my name for being a good Do-Bee. . .'

'Take it easy,' Denise told him. To Harold, she said, 'He's delirious. Go get a first-aid kit!'

As Harold ran off, Face glanced up at Denise and was mesmerised by her full, rounded lips. He knew his best chance of getting to know them better and went for it, making choking sounds and pointing weakly to his throat as if he wasn't able to draw in any air.

'He's having trouble breathing!' Denise said.

'Move aside,' Tony told her, dropping to his knees next to Face. 'He probably needs mouth to mouth. I know how to do it.'

Face turned his head and let loose with a loud cough that miraculously cleared his throat. Struggling to a sitting position, he wheezed, 'Ahhhh, I can breathe again! I can breathe! Thank God!'

'You're going to be all right,' Denise said, stroking a strand of damp hair from Face's forehead. 'Just lay back and take it easy, okay?'

As Tony stood back up and brushed sand off his knees, Face began to shudder. 'C-c-c-cold. I'm freezing.'

'Tony,' Denise told the Cuban, 'see if you can find a blanket up at the beach house. I'll try to keep him warm.'

'Okay.'

Tony headed off the same way Harold had, leaving Denise to take Face in her arms and hold him tightly. 'Is that better?' she asked.

'Much,' Face said.

As Denise reached over for her towel and then began to wipe the standing water from Face's tanned flesh, he smiled up at her.

'You're going to be okay,' she assured him.

'I have to tell you a secret,' Face confessed. 'You see, I wasn't really drowning.'

'What?' Denise stopped towelling him off and eyed him suspiciously.

'I just wanted to see you.'

'Is this a gag?'

'No, I'm serious.' Face sat up, showing Denise that he was as fit as could be. 'I know it was a lousy ploy, but I was desperate. You're a hard person to get close to. I mean, with all those bodyguards and everything. . .'

Denise's anger was quickly subdued by the flattery, and as she began to dry herself off with the towel, she asked Face, 'Do you know who I am?'

'I know you're one of the most beautiful creatures I've ever laid my eyes on,' Face said. 'Is that close enough?'

Denise frowned. 'I don't know about this. I get this feeling you're holding something back. . .'

Face looked over her shoulder. He couldn't see either of the bodyguards, but he knew he didn't have much more time. Gazing back at Denise, he reasoned, 'Hey, how many times have you gotten a napkin with a phone number on it from some guy at a restaurant? Or had some Romeo make eye contact with you on the street, looking to move in for a little time with you? Am I any different, aside from being more resourceful?'

'Well. . .'

'Give me a break,' Face pleaded. 'Don't I get any points for almost dying out there?'

Denise laughed, 'But you just told me you weren't really drowning.'

'A technicality.'

'Okay, I'll admit it *was* an original way of asking for a date,' Denise conceded. 'Unfortunately, you went to a lot of effort for nothing. You see, I already have a fella.'

Face shrugged, 'Hey, I didn't think this was gonna be easy.'

This time it was Denise that checked the beach to make sure Tony and Harold were nowhere in sight. Satisfied that they were still alone, she smiled at Face. 'Well, I might be able to get together with you for a drink. Maybe. My boyfriend's going out tonight.'

Where, Face wanted to know. He couldn't risk raising Denise's suspicions, however, so he tried approaching the question in a roundabout way. 'We wouldn't want to run into him, that's for sure.'

'He's got an important business dinner at the Waterfront Inn,' Denise divulged. 'How about if we meet around six at the Beachcomber? That's on the other side of the city.'

'That sounds great!' Face slowly rose to his feet, but he was a little wobbly.

'Hey, are you sure you're all right?'

Face nodded, bending over to massage his calves. 'My legs are just a little sore from all that dog-paddling.'

Harold and Tony finally came into view, bounding out of a beach house fifty yards away. Before they were within earshot, Denise quickly told Face, 'My name's Denise, by the way.'

'John,' Face said with a grin. 'As in Johnny Weismuller.'

He and Denise shared a quick chuckle as she helped him stay on his feet until the bodyguards returned with the first aid kit and blanket.

'Thank you so much,' Face told Tony as he accepted the blanket. 'You're a scholar and a gentleman. I don't think I need any first-aid, though.'

As Face wrapped the blanket around him, he cast a sidelong glance Denise's way and winked. She winked back. Harold noticed the exchange out of the corner of his eye, but he said nothing.

'You sure recovered fast,' Tony commented.

'What can I say?' Face exclaimed. 'I'm back in my element. Put both my feet on dry land and I won't have any trouble.'

'Yeah,' Harold mouthed cryptically, 'You're always better off when you don't go into anything over your head. . .'

'Right you are,' Face said, watching nervously as Harold picked up a piece of driftwood as thick as Face's arm and nonchalantly broke it in half.

'Firewood,' Harold explained.

'Of course,' Face said, swallowing hard.

14

The Waterfront Inn was a cosy, exclusive establishment located at the east end of Miami Beach. It had been built on the site of an old fishing wharf that had been flattened during the '26 hurricane, and the nautical motif was prevalent in the Waterfront's decor. In the restaurant, vintage fishnets hung from the ceiling, and the panelled walls were adorned with old anchors, lifesavers, and other assorted paraphernalia that had been sifted from the rubble of the original buildings. Portal windows opened to the sound of the sea and filled the dining room with a faint briny smell that lent even more atmosphere and was said to enhance the flavour of the seafood specialties that were the restaurant's claim to fame.

Joey Epic was sitting in a corner booth with an ocean view, accompanied by Kingsley and Jim the Cuban. Across from Joey sat a middle-aged man whose tasteful yachtsman attire was offset by a wretched toupee that looked as if he had gone wig-shopping at a carpet store and found a bargain in the remnant bin. He had a worried look about him, and when he tried to jam the filter of a fresh cigarette into an ivory holder, his hands were as unsteady as Joey's had been the previous day during his phone conversation with Boss Carlin of Chicago.

'Joey, do you think I'm crazy?' the man asked Epic. He finally managed to get the cigarette in place and lit it with a candle on the table. Through a cloud of smoke, he went on, 'Look what you've done for me all these years we've known each other. I can't believe you'd even think I would talk. . .'

'You'd be trying on concrete overshoes if you did, Councilman,' Joey said. 'Look, this Smith guy said he was onto us, and he had to get the dope from someone. I don't need to remind you what's at stake here. Michael, Mr Carlin put over fifty million into that high-rise we just built down the street. That's a lot of money.'

'I know, I know.' Councilman Bonitelli swilled down the last of his wine. Rocky refilled everyone's glasses from a chilled bottle of fine chablis.

'I hope you're telling me the truth, Michael,' Joey said, taking comfort at being the one who was giving someone else the shakes for a change.

'Joey, I swear,' Bonitelli said. 'I swear it!'

Joey picked up his wine glass and held it out before him. 'A toast.'

'To the new Las Vegas,' Bonitelli proposed. 'The new Atlantic City, right here in Miami Beach.'

The clinking of glasses rang like crystal chimes and everyone at the table sipped at their chablis as a busboy rolled a cart by the table and replaced the fat, half-burned candle in front of Bonitelli with a fresh one.

'Ah, could you tell our waiter we'll take our check now?' Joey asked the busboy.

'Yes, sir. . .'

'Wait a second. . .' Joey grabbed the busboy by the sleeve and looked him over. 'Don't I know you?'

The busboy froze. It was none other than Hannibal, disguised behind a paste-on moustache and a more convincing hairpiece than the one the Councilman was wearing. He smiled thinly at Epic. 'Perhaps you are thinking of my brother,' he suggested. 'He's a parking attendant at the Sunset Hotel.'

'Yeah, that must be it.' Joey let go of Hannibal. 'Listen,

instead of the check, why don't you have the dessert tray wheeled over here? I got a hankering for some coconut cream pie.'

'An excellent choice,' Hannibal said. He excused himself and quickly ducked into a side hallway, where he hurriedly changed out of the busboy jacket he'd borrowed from the laundry hamper just outside the kitchen door. As he was pocketing the candle he'd taken from Epic's table, a waiter emerged from the kitchen, holding a tray loaded with lobster dinners.

'When you get a chance, the guys by the window want to take a gander at the desserts,' Hannibal told him.

'And who are you?' the waiter sniffed contemptuously.

'Max Webern,' Hannibal improvised. 'Restaurant critic for the Sentinel. Nice place you got here. Good service, too.'

'Why, thank you!' the waiter beamed. 'My name is Anton. . .Anton Schonster. I have—'

'Nice to meet you, Anton, but I don't have time to chat. Deadline, you know.'

As Hannibal headed for the nearest exit, Anton called out, 'That's spelled S-c-h-o-n-s-t-e-r. . .'

Once outside the restaurant, Hannibal made his way to the parking lot, where B.A. was sitting behind the wheel of the idling Surfsider Hotel van. Face opened the back door for Hannibal and called out, 'Any luck?'

Getting into the van, Hannibal took the candle out of his pocket and twisted it until the base unscrewed, revealing a hollow space that had been filled with a microcassette recorder the size of a pregnant credit card. He pressed the rewind button, then played back a snippet of conversation between Joey and Councilman Bonitelli. 'This sounds a little muddy,' Hannibal said, 'but we can make out enough to get a lowdown on 'em.'

'Good goin', Colonel,' Murdock said.

'B.A.,' Hannibal called up to the front seat, 'let's go drop by the Councilman's house. I wanna be there by the time he's through with his pie and expresso. . .'

15

The salary for a Miami Beach Councilman was far from staggering, and yet Michael Bonitelli lived like a veritable king in a beachfront mansion surrounded by orange trees that filled the air with a citrus smell strong enough to overpower the oceanic aroma of the coastline. A horseshoe driveway arched its way up to the Colonial exterior of the house's front entrance, and as the distant chimes of St George's Church rang eleven times, Bonitelli pulled up in his custom Ferrari and parked. He got out of the car, whistling the chorus of the last song he'd been listening to on the radio. He hadn't taken more than three steps, however, before a tap on his shoulder turned his whistling to a gasp of fear. Whirling about, Bonitelli found himself facing B.A., whose aching jaw gave him an even fiercer countenance than usual.

'Please don't hurt me!' Bonitelli begged, raising his hands in the air. 'My wallet's in my jacket pocket. There's even a gold card you can have. Just don't—'

'Keep your wallet,' Hannibal said as he stepped out of the shadows and joined B.A. Face and Murdock followed close behind. 'We want *you*, Councilman.'

Murdock had his tourist outfit on, and for a change his camera had film in it. He turned up the brim of his hat so that he could press the camera against his face, then he snapped a quick picture of the bewildered man in the three-piece suit.

'Nice,' Murdock commented as he watched the photo that spat out the front end of his Polaroid and began to develop in the breezy night air.

'What's going on here?' Bonitelli demanded, mustering his courage.

'What a coincidence,' Face said, coming up behind Bonitelli and lowering the Councilman's arms, then posing with him for Murdock as if he and Bonitelli were long-time buddies. 'You see, that's what we were going to ask you.'

Hannibal took another step that brought him more into the light, then removed the disguise he had worn when retrieving the bugged candle at the Waterfront Inn. As Bonitelli stared in disbelief, Hannibal advised him, 'You should watch what you say over dinner, Councilman. You know the old saying, "Loose lips shrink ships."'

'That's "sink ships", Colonel,' Murdock corrected as he held his snapshots out at an angle to get a better look at them.

'Thank you, Murdock.' Hannibal showed Bonitelli the mini-recorder that had been used to tape his conversation, then signalled for B.A. to blindfold the Councilman with a strip of black cloth. 'We're going for a little ride, but it's not too scenic so we thought we'd spare you having to watch.'

'You're committing a federal offence here,' Bonitelli warned. 'If you're smart, you'll let me go and get the hell out of here. We can pretend this never happened.'

'Nice try, Councilman,' Hannibal said as he escorted Bonitelli back to the street, where the Surfsider van was parked halfway down the block. 'But we're just on our way to play a friendly little game of "Pin the Tail on the Donkey".'

'Yeah,' Face added, 'and the donkey's name is Joey Epic. . .'

Once Bonitelli was put inside the van, the others got in and remained silent as B.A. drove off, changing directions constantly to disorient the Councilman. Ten minutes later, the van drew to a stop near a deserted stretch of beach with a set of railroad tracks running through the sand.

'I can hear the ocean,' Bonitelli said as he was led from the van to the tracks by Hannibal and Face. B.A. and Murdock remained behind.

'How do you know it's the ocean?' Hannibal asked the blindfolded man. 'Maybe we're holding seashells next to your ears.'

'Forgive me if I don't appreciate your sense of humour,' Bonitelli drawled sarcastically.

'Gee, that's too bad,' Face said, 'because the gags are just starting. We were kinda hoping you'd get a kick out of this next one.'

Reaching the tracks, Hannibal and Face eased the Councilman down until he was laying across one of the ties like the farmer's daughter in an old B-movie. When Bonitelli's blindfold was removed and he realised what was happening, he cried out, 'This is crazy! Who are you?'

As he began tying Bonitelli's feet to the rails, Hannibal explained, 'Let's just say we're a group of concerned citizens. Kind of a "neighbourhood watch" club. Thanks to your little toast over dinner, we have a pretty clear picture of the scam you're brewing with Joey Epic.'

'I don't know what you're talking about!' The Councilman struggled to escape his captors, but B.A. arrived to hold him down while Face and Hannibal finished binding him to the tracks.

'Come on, Mikey,' Hannibal said. 'Wise up. You're pushing through a statute to allow gambling in Miami Beach, and Joey's trying to grab up as much beachfront property as he can so that he and Carlin will make a killing when it comes time to convert hotels into boardwalk casinos. You want me to go on?'

Bonitelli stopped struggling, but he still tried to sound as if he'd overcome his fears and was in control of the situation. He told Hannibal, 'You can't admit that tape in court.'

'Maybe you're right on that count,' Face interjected,

'but who said anything about going to court? This little stink of yours is just the sort of thing that newspapers like to stick their investigative reporters on. How long do you think it would take before they came up with enough headlines to shut down Joey and get you run out of town on a rail?'

Realising that he wasn't dealing with a handful of mindless thugs, the Councilman decided to change his tack. 'What do you want?' he asked calmly. 'What are you doing this for?'

'Kicks,' Hannibal said with a shrug, sitting down on the rail next to Bonitelli and lighting a cigar. 'Besides we have a couple of friends who didn't want to sell Joey their hotel. He threw a fit and gave them a hard time about it. You see, some people don't like the idea of opening this town up to the kind of scum that gambling tends to draw.'

'It seems to me your argument's with Epic, not me,' Bonitelli said. 'You don't have anything to gain by putting me through this. Come on, untie me, okay?'

Bonitelli's façade of calm reason lasted a few seconds, then was promptly shattered by the mournful howl of a train whistle sounding somewhere out in the distance.

'How about that?' Face looked at his watch. 'Right on time. Those folks at Amtrack sure know how to keep a timetable.'

'Get me off here!' the Councilman shouted vehemently. 'Get me off!'

Hannibal looked at Face, who removed a sheet of paper from his back pocket and handed it over. Hannibal puffed leisurely on his cigar as he squatted next to Bonitelli and said, 'We might be able to do that for you. . .provided you'd autograph this for us.'

'What is it?'

'A statement declaring that you won't vote in favour of any motion to rezone beach property or to introduce gambling in Miami Beach. We made a few calls before we picked you up, and it seems that you're the swing vote on these matters, and if you vote against 'em, the Council will, too.'

'I can't do it!' Bonitelli protested.

'Sure you can,' Hannibal said. 'I'll untie your right hand and give you a pen. B.A. here's a notary public, so it'll be nice and official. We tried to think of everything.'

'But I made a deal with Epic!' the Councilman wailed. 'If I double-cross him, I'm done for. He's a killer!'

'So's a three thousand ton train, from what I hear,' Face reminded him.

The train whistle sounded again, this time much closer. Soon a piercing headlight probed through the ocean mist, coming around the bend of the coast and bearing down on Bonitelli. The clatter of steel wheels rolling across rail joints grew louder as well.

'Untie me!' Bonitelli screamed above the pounding of the nearby surf. 'Help!'

'God helps those who help themselves,' Hannibal told the Councilman, waving the paper in front of him. 'What do you say?'

The train approached slowly, but showed no signs of stopping, and its relentless chugging sent Bonitelli's heart pounding against his chest. 'This is murder!' he shouted. 'You can't be serious about this!'

'Oh, we're serious, all right,' Hannibal said. 'Dead serious.'

Bonitelli craned his head and looked down the track. He could see the headlight inching closer through the light fog and feel the slight vibration of the rails underneath him. 'Okay, okay!' he yelled at Hannibal. 'I'll sign it! I'll sign anything!'

Face quickly untied the Councilman's right hand and gave him a pen. Bonitelli scrawled his signature across the bottom of the document, on the verge of hyperventilating in his fear. Face held the document up to the light of the oncoming train. 'Hmmmm, looks good to me. What do you think, B.A.?'

As B.A. took the document and looked it over, the Councilman howled, 'Get me up! Get me up!'

The train was now only a few dozen yards away, making so much noise it was hard for the men to talk without raising their voices.

'I don't know, Hannibal,' Face said, 'This guy is such a whiner.'

'I'll say.'

'My God, you can't leave me here to die!' Bonitelli was crying now. 'I signed it! You gotta save me!'

B.A. folded the paper up and put it in his pocket, declaring, 'This'll do the trick. Let's go!'

As B.A. headed back for the van, Hannibal and Face both glanced at the train, which was on the verge of materialising out of the haze, and Bonitelli, who had been reduced to a blubbering idiot on the tracks. When they simultaneously gave him a thumbs down, the Councilman bawled miserably, 'Noooooooooooo!!!!!'

When he looked up to meet his maker, Bonitelli suddenly stopped his sobbing. Instead of a train, all he saw rolling toward him was a hand-pumped rail car, and that came to a stop a few feet away from him. Murdock was working the pump from behind the stoplight mounted to the car's frame. A portable tape player blasted out the sound of a roaring train over its two powerful speakers. When Murdock turned off the player and doused the spotlight, it was as if Bonitelli had been awakened from a nightmare. He whimpered, a broken man, as Murdock hopped down from the cart and came over to begin untying him.

'I always wanted to do that!' Murdock enthused. 'Ever since I went on Mister Toad's Wild Ride at Disneyland. You know, where you go down that tunnel and that train comes right toward you? Whew, Fun City. . .and it doesn't even cost you an "E" ticket. . .'

16

By the time The A-Team returned with Bonitelli to his beachfront mansion, the Councilman had regained some of his composure. However, the prospects facing him once Joey Epic learned of his reversal on the rezoning and gambling measures gave him little cause for optimism about his future. As he was helped out of the Surfsider van and relieved of his blindfold, Bonitelli had the look of doom stamped on his pale features.

'I wish it would have been a real train,' he mumbled glumly. 'I'm finished.'

Murdock snapped Bonitelli's picture again, telling him, 'It was nice hanging out with you. Maybe we'll send you some of these shots if they turn out.'

'You're only finished around here,' Hannibal told him. 'Nothing's stopping you from packing your bags and hightailing it to someplace far from Joey's reach. That's your only chance, because you're never going to convince him you weren't talking to us all along.'

'Oh, I don't know about that,' Joey said from somewhere in the darkness. Before anyone in the van could react, floodlights bathed Bonitelli's front yard, revealing Joey and a dozen of his prized goons, all aiming various forms of firepower at the idling van.

'Floor it, B.A.!' Hannibal shouted as he and Murdock dived back in the van.

Before B.A. could shift gears however, the air filled with the sound of gunfire and all four of the van's tyres were ripped apart by a barrage of bullets. More than a few rounds also buried themselves in the vehicle's grille, piercing the radiator and fouling the engine until it died with a miserable sputter.

'The next volley goes a little higher!' Epic shouted at The A-Team. 'Get out and give up or you're all gonna have more holes than a doughnut shop.'

For several moments, there was no activity within the van. Bonitelli hurried away from the vehicle and took cover behind Kingsley and Jim the Cuban, who peered intently through the sights of their high-powered rifles while standing near the front walk. The Councilman looked over at Joey. 'Go ahead and give 'em the works! I'm going to relandscape the yard anyway. . .'

The doors of the van slowly swung open and The A-Team climbed out, unarmed, hands raised.

'Well, well,' Hannibal said, speaking around the cigar lodged between an unaffected grin. 'We certainly are spending a lot of time together, Joey.'

'We're going for a little ride,' Joey announced as his men moved in to frisk the Team.

'Thanks, but we just got back from one,' Face quipped. 'We'd hate to repeat ourselves. Tell you what, how about if you go ahead and we'll wait for you?'

'Try again, Pretty Boy.' Joey snapped his fingers and Rocky moved back behind a nearby shrub. When he reappeared, he had Denise with him. She was gagged and had her hands tied behind her back. As Rocky brought her over to join The A-Team, Joey told Face, 'You should be careful who you make dates with, especially when you stand 'em up. Denise has a very low threshhold for pain. She's soft on you guys and she talks real easy. You can let her keep you company until we're ready to flush you down the toilet.'

The A-Team was gagged as well, then escorted at

gunpoint to the row of limousines parked on the street. They were split up so that there were no more than two Team members in each vehicle and at least three armed men to keep an eye on each of them, including Denise. Nobody was about to try to buck the odds, and the limousines proceeded to the heart of Miami Beach without incident. Pulling off the main road, the limos rolled to a halt at a construction site where the framework for a new hotel was reaching up into the night. As the Team was dragged out of the limos and led into the basement of the skeletal building, Joey asked Hannibal, 'What do you think of it, Smith? Nice, huh?'

Hannibal couldn't speak through his gag, so he merely rolled his eyes.

The basement, like the rest of the hotel, was far from finished. Bare concrete walls, empty doorways, naked bulbs dangling from an exposed ceiling—it looked like the set for a Kafka festival. In the darkened corners, heaps of construction equipment were stored, waiting for work to resume on the hotel the following week. Once the Team was inside, Joey ordered his men to remove the gags, then told Hannibal, 'All right, so it looks a little rough around the edges at the moment.'

'My feeling exactly,' Hannibal said. 'But there's some definite potential here. Of course, without a gambling licence, you might have trouble drumming up much business, but why worry about trifles, eh?'

'That ordinance is going through,' Joey informed Hannibal. 'And once my good friend Mr Carlin has a look at things, he'll put up the money to finish this hotel and raze the Surfside so we can put up another new one. The only real snag we're facing now is that little slip of paper you twisted Bonitelli's arm to sign. Oh, yes, and he also said there's a tape you made of some dinner conversation at the Waterfront Inn. How about telling me where those little items are?'

'Joey, Joey,' Hannibal said, clucking his tongue as he shook his head. 'You should know by now that we aren't the chatty type.'

As his sidemen levelled their guns at the prisoners, Joey took a step forward and rammed a fist into Hannibal's side, adding new bruises to Smith's tender ribs. 'Cut the comedy, smartmouth!' Joey snapped. 'Look, the Councilman told us you made a stop on the way back to his place and got out of the van long enough to hide the tape and the paper. I'm not in the mood for a treasure hunt, so I'd advise you to spare me the trouble. Come clean and I might not end up using the whole lot of you for wallpaper paste. . .'

Hannibal remained bent over until the pain in his side eased, then he straightened up and eyed his foe with unflinching calm. 'Let me clear something up for you, Joey. You see, when we made that stop, only one of us got out and hid the evidence. . .and he didn't tell the others. You want to try to get some answers, you're gonna have to work us over one at a time, and even then it's not going to do you much good, because we come a little tougher than your girlfriend here. We're soldiers, pal, and you'll be lucky to get name, rank, and serial numbers. . .'

Joey was about to haul off and strike Hannibal again, but he thought better of it. His knuckles were still sore from the first blow and he figured it wasn't going to get him the results he was looking for anyway. He came up with a better idea, however, and told Rocky, 'Get over to the Surfsider and pick up those sisters! We'll see how tough Mr Smith and his boys want to play it when we start peeling off the girls' faces.'

'You're sick, Joey,' Hannibal said.

'No, I just like to have my way.' As Rocky headed out of the basement, Joey instructed the other men, 'Tie Denise and these guys up to the pillars, then lock 'em in here so they can think things over. . .'

'Joey, how can you do this to me!?' Denise cried out. 'After all I've done for you! I'm your girl!'

'That's history, doll,' Joey said. 'I can always get another. . .'

17

Hannibal and Murdock were tied to either side of one of the concrete pillars supporting the foundation ceiling; Face and Denise to another. B.A. was bound to a third pillar by himself. Moments after the basement door had been slammed shut on them, all the prisoners began to struggle against the thick cord that had been used to tie them.

'This is great!' B.A. snarled. 'My mouth is killin' me and I can't even reach it to put in some of that extract!'

'Forget about your tooth for the time being, B.A.,' Face called out. 'Can you bust your cord?'

'No, but I'd love to bust the chops of that fool Epic!'

'Wait a minute!' Denise said, rubbing her fingers against the pillar behind her. 'This cement hasn't been smoothed out. I can feel some ridges. Maybe if we keep chafing the cords against them, we can get out of this!'

'Hmmmm,' Face said rolling back against the pillar. 'Yeah, I feel a few spurs between my shoulder blades. You might be onto something there, Denise. Let's try moving in unison and see what happens.'

'Okay, but I don't know why I should be helping you, "John". I wouldn't be in this trouble if it wasn't for you, you know.'

'Wait and see. When this is all over, you'll be glad I lured you away from Joey,' Face said. 'He's no good for you. I mean, look how quickly he turned on you.'

'Hey, you two wanna debate some other time?' Hannibal called out. 'This pillar they tied me and Murdock to is smooth as a baby's butt. It's up to you guys. . .'

'Okay.' Face turned his head and was barely able to see Denise on the other side of the pillar. 'Shall we dance?'

Face and Denise began to wriggle in place, trying to work the cords against the concrete ridges. There wasn't much play in the cords, and after several minutes the two of them were sweating profusely, with little more to show for their efforts. . .or so they thought.

'This is hopeless,' Denise gasped as she caught her breath.

'We can't give up yet, Denise. Come on, let's. . .' Face stopped talking and began bobbing his head, fighting back a sneeze. It was a losing battle, however, and suddenly he let loose with a boisterous 'Ahhhhhhhhhchooooooo!!'

When it was over, Face found himself bounding away from the pillar, with the severed cords flopping down to the floor beside him.

'*Gesundheit!*' Hannibal said. 'I guess you were doing better than you thought, huh?'

Freed, Denise went over and began to work at the knots holding Hannibal and Murdock while Face untied B.A. from the other pillar.

'Now all we gotta do is find a way outta this basement,' B.A. said, rubbing his wrists as he strode over to the door through which they had been ushered into the basement. It was locked from the outside, and the hinges were also on the other side of the door. B.A. tried ramming it with his shoulder, but the door wouldn't give. 'Sucker's solid. We ain't gettin' through there without a key.'

'Maybe we won't have to,' Hannibal said, walking over to the far wall and looking over the equipment and supplies stacked there. In addition to various tools, there were boxes of ball bearings, safety flares, small cans of paint thinner, gallon buckets of latex and masonry paint,

91

and a crate filled with small glass jars among other items. 'B.A., come and have a look at this stuff. Seems to me that a little Yankee ingenuity might help us turn the tide.'

Murdock found the switch to throw a little more light on the materials, and as B.A. looked over the supplies, he gave his aching jaw another dose of cloves. Picking up one of the flares, he brought it to his nose and sniffed it the way Hannibal usually sampled the aroma of fine cigars.

'Yeahhhhh,' B.A. murmured, setting down the flare and looking over the glass jars and cans of thinner. 'I think I can whip up some grenades outta this, no problem.'

'That's what I like to hear.' Hannibal hoisted up a power jackhammer and tested its weight, then set it aside and looked over a stack of pipes with two-inch diameters. 'That hammer could come in handy, too, and my guess is these pipes are sturdy enough to be turned into makeshift bazookas.'

'Right you are, Hannibal,' Face said as he ran his fingers through a pail filled with thick, inch-long bolts. 'Joey Baby doesn't realise it, but he just locked us in a munitions plant. . .'

'You mean you're going to make weapons out of all these tools?' Denise asked, incredulous.

'Not all of 'em,' Hannibal told her. 'Just enough to give us a little leverage when your boyfriend comes back thinkin' he's got us by the tail.'

'He's not my boyfriend any more,' Denise insisted. 'I'm with you guys now. I want to help.'

'Good, because we've got our work cut out for us.' Hannibal summoned everyone together and quickly laid out a battle plan, then clapped his hands like a coach breaking up a huddle during the season championship. 'Okay, let's get down to it!'

B.A. tracked down a hacksaw and started carefully cutting into the flares, opening them up just enough so that he could pour out the flash powder into the small paint jars. After adding paint thinner and a handful of ball bearings to each of the jars, he handed them along to Murdock, who would punch a single hole in the lid before allowing Denise to apply the finishing touch, feeding a fuse-like cord into the hole. After a fumbling start, the trio of workers fell into a steady rhythm and began turning out the homemade grenades with assembly-line precision.

Meanwhile, Hannibal and Face were tinkering with the jackhammer. After dismantling the holding mechanism, they drilled out an inch-round hole in the piston guide and made a series of other adjustments that converted the tool's mean thrust into a means of propelling machine bolts, which Face then began to attach to rubber belts in the manner of ammunition clips used on precursors to the modern-day machine gun.

'If it doesn't backfire on us,' Hannibal decided, 'this baby oughta pack quite a punch. Hey, B.A., how's it coming on your end?'

'Grenades are ready,' B.A. reported, 'Now we're whippin' up a launcher!' For this, B.A. was removing the motor from a power saw and rigging it at the base of a length of pipe. Murdock held the pipe in place with one hand while he used the other to make sure the doctored paint jars would fit inside the pipe.

'Perfect!' he announced. 'With this little mother we'll be able to Bazooka Joey with no problem, right, B.A.?'

'Shut up and work, fool!'

Denise had found a set of blueprints for the building in the back corner, and after consulting with Hannibal and Face, the three of them went around and marked off spots near the bases of certain walls and pillars. When B.A. and Murdock had finished with the grenade launcher, they carried over a power drill and poked holes in the spots that had been made in the building's foundation. When the holes were completed, everyone chipped in, carefully inserting the makeshift grenades into the openings, then connecting all the jars with one long combustible fuse. When they were finished, the basement looked less like a storage area and more like a guerilla headquarters.

'Not bad for a rush job,' Hannibal had to admit as he surveyed the Team's handiwork. 'Now all we have to do is wait for Joey to show up for the free trial demonstration. . .'

18

Dawn was streaking the horizon with hazy hues of blue as the parade of limos returned to the construction site where The A-Team was being held captive. Once the vehicles were parked, doors opened and several tons' worth of human brawn and gunmetal poured out in the form of twenty armed men. As the small army spread out and took up firing positions surrounding the foundation of the half-built hotel, Joey Epic remained in his limo long enough to finish his car-phone conversation with Mr Carlin, who had arrived only moments before at Miami International on a non-stop flight out of Chicago. In the back seat, Sandy and Tina Conlon sat, dressed in the nightgowns they had been wearing when roused from sleep by their abductors.

'Mr Carlin, I'm tellin' you, it's done. I got the girls and those four men are as good as dead and buried. The war is over. We won, hands down.' As he listened to Carlin on the other line, Epic leered back at the women, basking in his anticipated triumph. 'Right, Mr Carlin. . .fine. I'll see you here in fifteen minutes and show you around. You're gonna like the looks of things, I promise you.'

As Joey hung up the car phone, Sandy told him, 'I don't see how you think you can get away with this!'

'You don't? Well, hang around and watch,' Joey

taunted as he got out of the front seat and opened the back door. 'You might learn something. Now get out!'

Sandy and Tina emerged from the limo and pulled their gowns tightly around them, staring at the ground to avoid the lascivious gazes of the men around them as Joey escorted them to the basement doorway. Jim the Cuban and Rocky flanked them on one side, Kingsley and Eddie on the other.

'Hey, Smith!' Joey shouted at the door as Kingsley stepped forward and fed a key into the lock. 'We have the girls. They're still in one piece, and if you wanna talk we can hold off pickin' em apart.'

There was no answer inside the basement. Kingsley sprang the lock and yanked the door open as Rocky and Eddie took aim through the darkened opening. Still nothing happened.

'We're waiting for an answer, Smith!' Joey said.

From within the basement, a strange, percussive series of sharp blasts sounded, and the men around Joey suddenly howled as they were pelted by hurtling bolts that packed the whallop of overgrown buckshot. A smoking flare rolled out into the doorway, providing a temporary screen through which The A-Team came charging out into the open, ready to do battle with Joey's minions.

'Here's your answer, Joey baby!' Hannibal shouted above the belching of the mutant jackhammer. 'I hope you choke on it!'

Epic shoved the Conlon sisters aside and bolted for the nearest cover, nearly bowling over Tony and Harold in the process. A shower of whizzing bolts pinged off the dumpster the three men were hiding behind. Harold showed himself long enough to squeeze off a round from his automatic, but his aim was reckless and succeeded only in scarring the hotel's foundation.

'Come on!' Denise hissed at Sandy and Tina from the basement doorway. 'Get inside!'

As the women took refuge inside the building, B.A. and Murdock dodged bullets and made their way to the nearby beach, carrying a box of the homemade grenades and the crude launcher. Setting up behind the cover of an overturned rowboat, Murdock started lighting fuses and dropping the potent paint jars into the launcher; then B.A. took aim at areas where he saw concentrations of Joey's men and sent the mini-bombs flying. Their explosive force rivalled that of conventional grenades, and half of Epic's force was taken out of the action by the first volley, which demolished one of the limos, reduced a stack of lumber into blazing splinters, and turned a patch of beach into a deep crater by displacing a storm of flying sand that temporarily blinded the men who had the misfortune to be looking in the direction of the explosion.

'Good shootin', B.A.!' Murdock cried out as he readied another batch of bombs. 'You win a Kewpie doll of your choice!'

B.A. grimaced and grunted, rubbing his cheek. When bullets began dancing along the hull of the boat, he ducked down. 'They ain't slouches themselves!'

From behind the dumpster, Joey fired his revolver at Hannibal and Face, who had propped up the jackhammer on the hood of a bulldozer and began swinging it from side to side to direct a steady spray of bolts out the enemy.

'I shoulda wasted 'em when I had the chance,' Joey berated himself between shots. 'Look at the mess they're makin' around here!'

'Forget the mess, boss!' Harold told him. 'We're gettin' our butts kicked!'

Indeed, a handful of Joey's men, led by Tony, had already had their fill of ball-bearing bombs and stinging bolts. They made a mad dash for one of the remaining limos and piled in. Tony started up the engine and slammed the gears into reverse, backing around the smouldering, twisted carcass of the limo that had taken a direct hit from one of The A-Team's paint-jar specials. As Tony shifted into first and floored the accelerator, Hannibal took aim with the jackhammer and Face pulled the makeshift trigger. Bolts spewed from the weapon and glanced at an angle off the limo's front windshield, webbing the glass enough to foul Tony's view. Losing control of the vehicle, Tony veered the limo wildly to one side and it sped up the incline of a toppled lumber pile and ploughed sideways into a tool shed with so much force that the front end of the limo wrinkled like an accordion. Once the car plopped onto the sand, the doors slowly opened and the stunned occupants staggered out, waving their arms in surrender.

Joey could sense that his brief reign as princepin of Miami Beach was being nipped in the bud before his eyes. All he could hope to do now was try to escape with his skin intact and keep running until he found some dark hole he could hide in where the Cardenac Brothers wouldn't be able to find him. As he emptied his revolver at the bulldozer from behind which Hannibal and Face were spitting hot bolts, Epic saw Rocky sneaking out into the water behind the hotel and then climbing into a moored speedboat.

'Keep me covered!' Joey ordered Tony and Harold. 'I'm gonna try to circle around and sneak up behind those guys shootin' grenades at us!'

Tony and Harold tried to follow orders, but within seconds after Joey had left them, a ball-bearing bomb went off a dozen feet in front of them, flipping the dumpster in the air and showering them with enough debris to take the fight out of them.

Taking advantage of the distraction, Joey took long strides and reached the docks just as Rocky was revving the boat's motor. Hopping into the craft, Joey hurriedly untied the mooring ropes and shouted, 'Let's get outta here, Rocky!'

Rocky leaned on the throttle and backed the speedboat out into deeper water, then pushed the motor to its limit as he pointed the ship's prow out toward the stretching blue of the Atlantic.

It was all over on the mainland, as Joey's battered legions were no longer willing to risk life and limb, especially when their boss was deserting them. Denise, Sandy, and Tina emerged from the basement and picked up a few fallen weapons, using them to hold the thugs under cover while The A-Team turned its attention to the fleeing speedboat.

"'Ohhhh, say can you see, by the dawn's early light!'" Murdock sang as he slipped the last two jar-bombs into the pipe launcher.

'Yeah, I see 'em, sucker!' B.A. said, shifting the pipe to take aim.

"'And the rockets' red glare!'" Murdock howled, watching the launched jars thump out over the ocean. "'The bombs bursting in air. . .make that bursting in water!'"

In quick succession, the bombs rocked the surface of the water in front of the boat, sending spray flying up into the faces of Joey and Rocky. When Hannibal and Face followed up with a surge of bolts from their trusty jackhammer, the boat went as much out of control as the limo had earlier, and by the time Rocky climbed back up from hitting the deck, he and Joey gaped with horror to see that they were heading back toward the shoreline. They tried to abandon the runaway craft, but it was too late. With a jarring thud, the boat bounded ashore and took to the air for a good dozen yards before crash-landing in the sand.

'Well, hello, Joey, well, hello, Joey!' Murdock crooned as he and B.A. apprehended Epic and Rocky, 'It's so nice to have you back where you belong. . .'

'Shut up!' Joey moaned as he was helped from the crunched hulk of the beached speedboat.

'Hey, for once I agree with you,' B.A. told the gangster. Elbowing his sidekick, he seconded, 'Shut up, fool!'

As the rest of The A-Team helped the women round up the prisoners, Hannibal lit up a cigar and vanished briefly inside the basement of the hotel. When he returned, he was reeling out a length of cable behind him. 'Well, Joey,' he told the thugs' leader when he rejoined the group, 'Thanks for the workout. To show our appreciation, we thought we'd put on a little fireworks display.'

Seeing Hannibal touch the tip of his cigar to the end of

the cable, Joey's eyes bulged. 'What are you doing? What is that?'

When the cable began to burn down with a rapid hiss, Hannibal informed Joey, 'I think they call it a fuse. Now, if you're smart, you and everyone else here will hit the proverbial deck. . .'

With haste, the congregation on the beach scrambled away from the hotel and dove to the sand. A few people summoned the nerve to peek back at the hotel, and they were treated to one of the more impressive phenomena in the construction industry. Over the space of a few fleeting seconds, a series of muffled explosions sounded from within the basement, and a cloud of smoke gushed out of the opened doorway. Then, in a matter of only a few more seconds, the massive structure of the hotel roared and crumbled in on itself, imploding like some inflated toy that had its plug removed.

'Ah, I love it when a plan comes together,' Hannibal said.

'And I love it when a building comes apart,' Face added.

As a billowing mass of smoke rose from the rubble of the fallen hotel, The A-Team got up and brushed the sand from their clothes, then held guns on Joey's mob as they did the same. Joey's jaw hung slack and he made pitiful whimpering sounds as he looked at the ruins, unable to articulate the full extent of his anguish.

'Don't take it so hard, Joey,' Murdock told him. 'The colour was all wrong, anyway.'

'Lousy construction,' Face opined, 'I hear you paid off a lot of inspectors, Joey Baby.'

Sirens began to sound in the distance. More closely, a lavish Rolls Royce pulled off the main road and came to a stop near the wreck of one of the limos. As Mr Carlin lifted his weighty girth out of the sedan, Denise quickly approached him and poked her gun at his midsection. Hannibal took aim at the mobster's bodyguards and Face covered the chauffeur.

'You can gawk all you want, but no fancy moves,'

Hannibal advised.

'My hotel!' Carlin gasped, staring at the destruction. 'My hotel! What happened to my hotel?'

'Maybe you should ask Joey,' Hannibal grinned. 'Welcome to Miami Beach. . .'

19

'Hey, get a load of this!' Face said, looking up from a specially delivered copy of the previous day's LA Courier-Express. He sat by the Surfsider's pool with the rest of The A-Team, who had closed off the area for a few hours so they could privately recuperate from the morning's ordeal.

'What's that?' Hannibal asked without bothering to open his eyes. He was floating on his back on an inflated raft, trailing his toes in the refreshing water of the pool.

'It says here there's been some changes made at my old orphanage,' Face told the others as he skimmed through the article in the paper. 'Apparently they're beefing up the school's curriculum to get better accreditation. Not only that, but they're also changing the name from St Bartholomew's to St Mary's and reactivating the athletic programme. Hey, that's great! I think they bailed out of sports competition a few years after I left.'

'Maybe they need some coaches,' Hannibal snickered as he bumped into the side of the pool and pushed back off into deeper water.

'Yeah!' Face said. 'You know, I think I'd like to check that out!'

'Hey, I was just kidding, Face,'

'But I'm not.' Face looked over at B.A., who sat at the pool's edge with his feet in the water. He had an ice bag pressed against the side of his face and looked miserable. 'Hey, B.A. what do you say we pay 'em a visit once we get back to LA and try to breathe a little life into a football team? You'd love the kids there, I guarantee it.'

'Man, when we get back to LA, the first place I'm gonna visit is that dentist friend of yours,' B.A. complained. 'I'm gonna give him the choice of either getting rid of this pain in my mouth or havin' me do some work on *his* teeth!' B.A. slammed his fist into the water to indicate the sort of finesse work he had in mind for Dr Kalalau.

Murdock was off by himself, practicing shuffleboard and humming to himself. He suddenly stopped playing, though, and sniffed the air. 'Mmm, boy, do I smell some good groceries!'

The gate of the pool area swung open and the Conlon sisters wheeled in two carts filled with servings of fresh fruit, crabmeat and shrimp cocktails, chips and salsa, four sizzling steaks, and a few ice buckets filled with bottles of the hotel's best champagne.

'Soup's on, guys!' Sandy chimed.

Face set down the paper and looked over the offerings brought before him. 'Some soup. . .'

'We told the chefs to pull out all the stops,' Tina said as she started transferring the dishes to a poolside table already prepared with table settings for the group. 'It's the very least we could do for you after what you've done for us.'

'Hey, for a Florida getaway as nice as this, it was worth it,' Hannibal said as he hand-paddled his way to the edge of the pool and climbed out of the water. He sampled one of the shrimps and closed his eyes, smiling with satisfaction. 'Keep spoiling us like this and we might never leave.'

'That would be fine with us,' Sandy confessed. 'We like having you around.'

'Well, with Joey out of commission and Bonitelli too scared to go against us again, you shouldn't have any more problems running things here by yourselves,' Hannibal told them. 'If you do, all you have to do is call and we'll be on the next plane. . .'

'Speak for yourself, Hannibal!' B.A. advised. As he headed for the table, B.A. paused to pick up the sports section of the Courier-Express. He was browsing through the standings when his eyes suddenly widened and he dropped the icebag to the ground. 'Hannibal! What's this jive!???'

'Oh, oh,' Hannibal muttered, seeing B.A.'s temper bloom like a weed in hot weather. 'The gig's up.'

'Man, this paper's dated the ninth!' B.A. said hotly.

'It's an old paper,' Face offered lamely.

B.A. grabbed Sandy's wrist and checked the watch she was wearing. 'Just a day old. Today's the tenth! That means I got here in just a day.'

'So, what's a day or two among friends?' Face asked.

'I didn't get here in no car man!' B.A. looked accusingly at Murdock. 'You tricked me, sucker!'

'Don't look at me like that B.A., ol' buddy.' Murdock held his shuffleboard stick before him like a hockey player looking to spend time in the penalty box. 'I'm a soldier. I was just following orders. . .'

'I'm gonna add you to the chip dip, Murdock!'

'Aw, B.A, have a heart,' Murdock pleaded. 'I'm not into salsa!'

'You will be soon!'

When B.A. charged him, Murdock threw a quick cross-check with the shuffleboard stick, dazing Baracus momentarily with a light blow to the jaw. Gaining a few precious seconds, he turned heel and headed for the beach, telling Hannibal and Face, 'Keep my steak warm. I'll be right back. . .I hope!'

'You're done for, fool!' B.A. shouted as he took up the chase.

There was some sort of commotion on the beach, and a few dozen people gathered near the water's edge were shouting to one another and occasionally pointing out at the waves, which were deserted save for a Coast Guard cutter that bobbed up and down in the choppy waters. When Murdock barrelled past a group of onlookers and headed into the water, a few people reached out to grab him, but he twisted away from them and dived headlong into the surf.

'My God!' a woman shrieked, pressing the sides of her head as she watched Murdock. 'He'll kill himself.'

'He sure will,' B.A. said as he rushed past. 'Damn fool can't swim!'

'No, I mean there's a shark out there!' the woman wailed.

B.A. ground to a halt and looked back at the woman. 'What'd you say?'

'A shark!' she repeated. 'A Great White! Look! There it is!'

B.A. gazed out where the woman was pointing and saw the triangular fin cutting through the water, heading for where Murdock was slogging through the surf, less than fifty yards away.

'Oh, man. . .!' B.A. saw a long piece of driftwood lying in the sand and grabbed it as he headed out into the water, shouting, 'Murdock! Get back here!'

Spluttering as he thrashed at the water to keep afloat, Murdock saw the crude club in B.A.'s hand and took a deep breath before diving under an oncoming wave and heading out for deeper water, oblivious to the cries from people on shore and in the Coast Guard warning him about the shark.

Fortunately, even despite the burdensome weight of his gold chains and jewellery, B.A. was a stronger and more skilful swimmer than Murdock. While Murdock started to be pushed back inland by the play of the waves, B.A. was able to swim against the flow and close the distance between him and his colleague, all the while retaining a hold on the gnarled length of driftwood. Fifty yards out was a sandbar, and when he realised that he could touch bottom and still have his head and shoulders above the water, B.A. stopped swimming and shouted for Murdock to do the same, adding, 'There's a shark comin' after you, sucker!'

'You're just trying to trick me!' Murdock cried above

104

the slapping of the waves, refusing to give up his feeble attempts to outswim B.A. It was only when he saw that B.A.. had turned his back to him and raised his club above his head to face something coming from the other direction that Murdock noticed the shark's fin, now closing in on B.A..

'Oh, no, it's Jaws!' Murdock gasped. 'B.A., watch out!'

B.A. was ready. He waited until the last possible second, then slammed down the club as hard as he could against the blunt nose of the attacking shark. It was a direct hit, and although B.A. was bowled over by the creature's mighty tail, the shark veered away from its human targets and fled past the Coast Guard ship for deeper water.

'B.A.!' Murdock shouted, touching down on the sand bar and wading toward the spot where his friend had disappeared below the surface. When he could see no trace of B.A., Murdock began to panic. 'Come on, big guy! Lemme see that ugly mug of yours again and I'll help you thrash mc all you want! You saved me, B.A.! You're my hero! B.A.! Where are you?!!!'

'Right behind you, you crazy fool!'

Murdock practically jumped out of the water with fright. B.A. caught him and turned him around so they were facing one another.

'Oh, B.A.! The Baracian One has survived! Hallelujah!'

'Say what?'

Murdock's eyes glistened with near religious fervour as he beheld his saviour. 'I am yours to do with as you please, B.A.. Spit on me, ground me with equal parts of guacamole. . .'

'Put a lid on it, fool!' B.A. growled. 'Man, all that swimmin' musta left you with water on the brain. You're talkin' crazy!'

Nonetheless, Murdock continued to heap adulation on B.A. all the way back to shore, where the astonished crowd eyed both men with wonder. When they started to rush over to bombard B.A. with questions about his incredible duel with the shark, Murdock kept them away with a wave of his hands, shouting, 'Please! No questions! No comment! The Baracian One does not wish to be bothered. Make way, make way!'

'Come on, Murdock!' B.A. said, grabbing him by the arm and dragging him back to the pool area, where the Conlon sisters stood with Face and Hannibal at the vantage point offering the best view of the ocean. They had all obviously seen what had happened, and as the women hurried over to Murdock and B.A. with towels, Hannibal quickly poured two glasses of champagne and handed them to the drenched men.

'You two sure know how to put on a show for the natives.'

'Nice move with that club, B.A.,' Face added. 'Maybe you can coach St Mary's baseball team, too.'

Murdock took a sip of his champagne, then chastised Hannibal and Face, 'How dare you belittle the feats of the Baracian One!'

'The Baracian One?' Face questioned.

B.A. shrugged his shoulders, then twirled a finger in orbit around one ear as he said, 'Fool's got a new screw loose.'

'Listen, B.A., how's your mouth doing after all that excitement?' Hannibal asked.

An amazed expression came over B.A.'s face as he worked his jaw back and forth, then up and down. 'Hey, I don't believe it! The pain's gone, man!'

Hannibal held his hand out and opened his palm, revealing a tooth. 'Dr Murdock took this out for you with that shuffleboard stick before you chased him into the ocean. I guess maybe you must have had two bad ones instead of just the one Doc Kalalau got.'

'All right!' B.A. took the tooth from Hannibal and showed it to Murdock. 'Hey, that makes us even as far as I'm concerned.'

'Oh, never, oh Baracian One!' Murdock bowed before B.A. and declared, 'I am at your service forever and still I won't be able to repay the debt I owe you.'

'Oh yeah?' B.A. said. 'In that case, I got an idea. After

we. finish eatin' and packin', we'll go down to the rental place and check out a nice station wagon, then *you* can drive *me* all the way back to Los Angeles. . .and I'm gonna stay awake the whole time if I gotta to make sure you don't try to knock me out and stick me on a plane!'

20

Instead of a station wagon, The A-Team ended up renting the plushest van they could get their hands on for their cross-country trip back to Loss Angeles. With their share of the profits from the Surfsider's upswing in business, the Team outfitted the vehicle with a few additional amenities, such as a custom tape player and a few dozen cassettes, foam pads to use for beds in the back, and enough foodstuffs to store in a portable refrigerator for long jaunts on the road. Once everything was in readiness, they bade a fond farewell to the Conlon sisters and set out on the nearest interstate. In no great hurry, the Team established a leisurely pace, taking turns behind the wheel and giving themselves eight days for the journey, making several stops along the way to check up on old acquaintances and former clients they'd done business with over the past years. Between visits, the steady lull of the freeway provided them with the relaxation they had been largely denied in Miami Beach, and by the time they had arrived back on their home turf, the Team felt well-rested and ready to take on a fresh challenge. They put out word through the LA underground that their services were once again available, but, remarkably, the days went by without anyone tracking down the enigmatic Mr Lee or some other connection with a tale of woe and a request for the particular expertise of The A-Team. To dispel what was quickly becoming a severe case of boredom, Face convinced the Team to join him in dropping by his old alma mater, the newly christened St Mary's Orphanage Academy. As it turned out, the nuns of St Mary's were facing a plight that, in the absence of other offers, struck The A-Team as a cause worthy of their best effort.

It seemed that St Mary's had been able to wrangle its way onto the football schedule with a number of area schools, only to have the entire coaching staff come down with a severe strain of viral influenza the week before the season opener. Face was quick to volunteer the Team to fill the temporary void, and with a little arm-twisting, the others agreed to pitch in. While Face took on duties as head coach in charge of the St Mary's offence, B.A. took command of the defence, and both Hannibal and Murdock consented to lend a hand with whatever else needed doing.

Within three days, Face and B.A. had developed a fierce rivalry, pitting their youthful squads against one another in daily scrimmages taking place on the recently renovated football field behind the Academy's Old Mission-style buildings. The first day, Face had run his offence with some razzle-dazzle plays featuring the talents of quarterback phenom Billy Rey, a black teenager with definite potential. Although that first contest had been a one-sided victory for the offence, B.A. had buckled down and beefed up his defensive forces the following day to blunt Face's squad from gaining more than a handful of hard-fought yards the entire practice session. And so now came the rubber scrimmage, with both sides taking to the field with all the determination and inspiration their respective coaches could drill into them.

Face drew his boys into a tight huddle in the shade cast by the nearby bell tower. All the players were wearing new white jerseys with the school name lettered on the back, save for Billy Rey, who wore a plain red shirt. As he divvied out instructions, Face dragged a finger tip across his palm to illustrate the plays.

'Look, Miller, it's a brush block. Don't nail the defensive end, okay? Drift out to the left flat. . .pulling guard and halfback's sweep right. Build the pocket. Rey pumps once to the right and then fires back. This play depends on deception. Nobody look to the left; don't tip our hand. . .'

Twenty yards away, B.A. was holding his own huddle in the blazing sun, grinning as he looked at Face going through his coaching motions. 'Faceman, he likes deception plays,' he told his defensive players, who all wore dark jerseys. 'Only problem is, deception plays ain't gonna work on my defence. . .'

'Aren't,' one of the players corrected B.A.

'Say what?' B.A. asked the youth.

'You should say "aren't" instead of "ain't", Mr Baracus.'

'Yeah, and you should call me Coach instead of Mr Baracus,' B.A. shot back before resuming his pep talk. 'Now, then, the basic premise of our defence is gonna be that nobody's gonna deceive ya if he's sittin' on his butt! So I want all of you to go out there and get these uniforms dirty! All right?'

'All right!' the defensive squad cheered, breaking their huddle and taking up positions on their side of the scrimmage line.

Over on the sidelines, Hannibal and Murdock watched on, having gladly restricted their input to handling equipment and tending to any first-aid that might be needed during the course of the practice sessions.

'I hate to say it,' Hannibal told Murdock, 'but I think Face might have jumped in over his head here. These guys'll never be able to play a triple-A school like Banning High.'

'Yes, yes,' Murdock agreed, bobbing his head as if he had a spring for a neck. He had yet to stabilise fully from the shark incident, and his eyes were still slightly glazed with a hint of fanaticism. His voice, too, rang with an enthusiasm totally out of proportion with the gist of his conversation. 'The Faceman has gotten in over his head.

Yes, he has. He really has. But still. . .' His eyes rolled upward, taking in the tower, with its cluster of patina-laden bells. 'Still, there is always the power of prayer. . .'

'Whatever you say, Murdock.' Hannibal smirked as he lit his cigar and watched as both sides lined up on the field for the next play.

Billy Rey crouched behind the offensive centre and looked to both sides to make sure his team was in position, then barked a few signals before being awarded with a quick snap of the pigskin. As he backpedalled from the scrimmage line, B.A.'s defensive powerhouse laid seige to the offence with a vengeance. Young Miller was promptly deposited on his keister and half the offence joined him on the turf, weighed under by opposing team-mates. The would-be pocket never materialised, and Billy Rey was quickly hauled down by a blitzing mob of defensive linemen.

'What are you doing!' Face shrieked, blowing his whistle as he ran back onto the field. 'Get off! Get off him, for cryin' out loud!'

While Face helped his beleaguered offence to his feet, B.A. chortled and clapped his hands as he cheered on the defence. 'Way to hit! Good goin'! Okay, okay, okay!'

'That does it!' Face stormed over to B.A. and the two coaches faced off, nose-to-nose. 'This is a scrimmage, Baracus! A scrimmage! A scrimmage is an exercise to try to work out timing. It is considered highly advisable that in a scrimmage you don't try to kill your own quarterback!'

B.A. sneered back at Face and laughed, 'Your guys should be wearin' dresses, Face!'

'Are you listening to me, B.A.? You don't try to put the team's only offensive weapon on the disabled list a few days before the first game of the season.'

B.A. shrugged. 'What can I say, man? My guys eat offences for breakfast. We came to play. . .'

As B.A. wandered off, Face fumed and summoned his troops back into a huddle. Resorting to his clipboard, he hastily scribbled out one of the plays he remembered having good results with during his own playing days.

'Okay, if he wants power football, we can play power football, right, guys?'

'Right, coach!' the offence responded.

'Good,' Face said. 'Then we're gonna hit 'em with the ol' Twenty-eight Blast. We went over this yesterday, remember? Right on two.'

'Got it,' Billy Rey said.

From their sideline perspective, Hannibal and Murdock continued to view the proceedings. Between puffs on his cigar, Hannibal conceded, 'B.A.'s shaping up the defence pretty well.'

'Oh, undeniably,' Murdock gushed. 'I mean, just take a look at the Baracian One, Hannibal, out there firing up those little buggers. Why, he's turning those boys into men, Colonel. B.A. is molding futures and. . .well, sir, I for one am beginning to see him in another light.'

'Another light. . .right, Murdock.' Hannibal looked to the sky. 'Well, it's after four o'clock and, yes, the light *is* changing. Things always look different at twilight. It'll all be back in focus for you again tomorrow maybe, huh?'

· 'I don't think so, Colonel,' Murdock said sombrely as he gazed admiringly at B.A., 'What I'm seeing out there on that field is something I've never seen before. I'm seeing human courage, sir. I'm seeing a builder of men. Knute Rockne. . .Vince Lombardi. . .these were true leaders, sir, unlike the ones I've been exposed to, and I think the Baracian One is cut from the same noble cloth. Yes, sir, I truly do. . .'

Hannibal's lower lip sagged visibly at the comment. He removed his cigar and grappled with his feelings of hurt at Murdock's comment. 'You know, there were times in Nam when I. . .I mean, leadership comes in many colours, Murdock. Many shades. . .many *lights*. . .'

Murdock was so caught up in his reverence that he missed Hannibal's point and waved away the other man's remarks. 'B.A. is a true leader, sir. He's a man who can inspire others. He can inject into those boys a noble purpose.'

'Kill those suckers!' B.A. shouted to his young defence

as he broke up their huddle and moved away from the playing field to the sidelines opposite from where Hannibal and Murdock were standing. When Murdock waved excitedly at him, B.A. returned the gesture with appreciably less enthusiasm.

'Let me give you an example of what I'm saying, sir,' Murdock told Hannibal. 'You know that tattoo on B.A.'s arm? The one that says T.C.B.?'

'Know it?' Hannibal scoffed. 'I was with him when he had it put on. We were in Saigon, celebrating a furlough—'

'Yes, yes,' Murdock interrupted impatiently, 'but back to my point. Well, sir, for the longest time I thought that was a really silly thing. "Taking Care of Business". . .what did that mean, I always wondered. It seemed so trite, even stupid. But now. . .now I am really seeing what it is. Out here, before our very eyes, the Baracian One is truly taking care of business.'

Hannibal took a deep breath, wondering how much longer this latest phase of Murdock's would go on. For some time, apparently, because when the resumption of play resulted in another trouncing of the offence and sacking of Billy Rey, Murdock whistled with unabashed awe and applauded until his hands were sore.

'The man is simply taking care of business, Colonel. Are you seeing what I'm saying?'

'Do I have a choice?' Hannibal wondered. Trying to hide both his annoyance and disappointment, he asked, 'He's really become a hero to you, hasn't he, Murdock?'

'Not *a* hero, Colonel,' Murdock corrected. '*The* hero. This man has a courage and power that, if applied correctly, can change lives.'

'Gee, maybe we should put him in a bottle and sell him,' Hannibal said. To himself, he began to wonder if this diversion at the Academy was turning out to be such a wise venture. Face and B.A. were at each other's throats, Murdock was practically on his knees worshipping B.A., and he was feeling the itch for some of the kind of action that made the Team function like a true unit. What he felt everyone could use was a good shot of the jazz. . .

21

The kind of trouble Hannibal was used to dealing with was brewing closer to home than he anticipated.

Less than a long punt away from the football field, two men who looked like refugees from Joey Epic's gang of cut-throats watched the scrimmage with keen interest through binoculars. They were in the parking lot overlooking the field, peering out through the cover of an overgrown lilac bush that had them smelling as if someone had switched their deodorant with bottles of body perfume for women.

'Practice is over, finally,' the taller of the men said, lowering his binoculars. He turned to his partner. 'Let's slap that transmitter on Billy Rey's car and get outta here before this damn smell knocks me out!'

'You got it, Ryack,' the shorter man said, wrinkling his nose with distaste as he backed out of the bush. 'Man, the missus takes one whiff of me and she'll be after me with the rolling pin, you can count on it. . .'

There were only a few vehicles in the parking lot, including the unmistakable black van belonging to B.A. After checking to make sure the coast was clear, Ryack and the short man padded quickly across the asphalt to an old Chevy Nova parked in the shade of a tall pine tree. As the short man stood watch, Ryack removed a small box from his coat pocket and pried open the lid. Inside was a small magnet-backed transmitter, which he carefully took out and slipped into place under the rear bumper of the Nova. After pulling out the short antenna on the transmitter, he looked over the bumper from several positions to make sure no one could accidentally spot the bug.

'Okay, Mike,' Ryack said, stuffing the empty box back in his pocket. 'Now let's go pay Billy boy a little visit and refresh his memory about a few things.'

'Sure thing.'

As the men headed back across the parking lot, they both lit up cigarettes and started blowing smoke on each other to combat the floral scent clinging to them from their vigil in the lilac bush. A steep concrete staircase led down to the fieldhouse, an old brick building shrouded with ivy and bougainvillaea. They stole to the corner and watched as the football squad jogged into the fieldhouse. Billy Rey hung back from the others, pausing every few steps to rub a bruise on his thigh he'd received the last time he'd been tackled. Once the quarterback was within earshot, Ryack leaned out from the cover of the bourgainvillaea and whispered, 'Pssssst! Billy Rey!'

When he spotted Ryack, Billy froze, and for a moment it looked as if he was going to turn around and say something to B.A., who was following a few dozen yards behind, engrossed in an argument with Face. However, when Ryack shook his head and made a slicing gesture across his throat, Billy swallowed hard and moved around the corner of the building. Ryack grabbed him and pulled him in close to the wall as Face and B.A. walked past, heading into the fieldhouse.

'What I want, B.A.,' Face was arguing, 'is to get a chance to work on some timing patterns. I deliberately put a red shirt on Billy Rey so he wouldn't get hit and what happens? He spends the afternoon on his back!'

'I coach to win, man!' B.A. asserted. 'If your guys can't take the heat in a scrimmage, how do you expect 'em to be tough enough to hold up in a game situation? Huh? It's gonna be dog-eat-dog against Banning, and if we're gonna be the top dog, we gotta be ready for some rough and tumble!'

One of the younger nuns was in the fieldhouse hallway, cleaning the trophy case. As Face and B.A. passed, she intercepted them, brimming with excitement. 'Oh, Templeton, isn't this grand? Sports being a big thing again at the orphanage. . .why, you can't believe what a boost it's been for the kids, boys and girls alike. And we owe it all to you and your friends. . .'

'Well, now, Sister Catherine,' Face said modestly, 'we're just stepping in here temporarily. . .'

'But you're putting your heart and soul into it, Templeton, and that counts for a lot.' Sister Catherine pointed through the case at a handful of trophies and team pictures. 'You had a hand in our winning half of these awards when you were here,' she reminded Face, 'and it's only fitting that you should be the one to help start us back on our winning ways!'

'I sure hope so, sister,' Face said.

B.A. leaned close to the case, eyeing one of the team pictures. He began to laugh. 'Hey, there you are, Face! You sure were a skinny little runt back then. How'd you ever get to be such a star?'

'Grit and determination,' Face boasted.

'Aha!' B.A. said. 'And I bet you busted your butt in practice and always played for keeps, right?'

'He sure did,' Sister Catherine affirmed. 'And now he's going to help us clobber those creeps at Banning High on Saturday, right, Templeton?'

'Banning?' Face said. 'Oh, well, Banning. . .they were division champs last year after all and. . .well. . .Banning is tough. Yes, ma'am, sister, no doubt about that. . .'

Sister Catherine sighed nostalgically. 'I remember when you were playing here, Templeton. If was my first year here, and I practically had a crush on you. You were so graceful. . .the way you would stand back there with no fear and throw those wonderful passes. So marvellous. . . so heroic.'

Face blushed, but not enough to keep himself from getting caught up in the same memories. 'Well, I was pretty good, wasn't I?'

'I think I'm gonna be ill,' B.A. groaned under his breath.

Sister Catherine came back to the present and told Face, 'And you say Billy Rey has the talent to be a big star, too, so we're counting on a victory. We know you won't let us down.'

Either the nun's enthusiasm was infectious or else Face was putting on a bold front, because he shook off his pessimism and clapped his hands together decisively, declaring, 'Don't worry about Banning, Sister Catherine. The bigger they are, the harder they fall.'

'You got it wrong, man,' B.A. countered, 'The bigger they are, the harder they hit. . .'

Before B.A. and Face could resume their argument, Billy stepped into the hallway and cleared his throat. Face looked over and asked, 'Hey, Billy, why aren't you in taking a shower? Is that thigh still acting up?'

'Excuse me, coach, but I need to talk to you a minute,' Billy said. 'It's important.'

'Sure, Billy,' Face told him, 'Come on, there's nobody in the fieldhouse. Sister Catherine, keep up the team spirit. B.A., tell Hannibal and Murdock I'll be ready to go in a bit.'

As Face led Billy into the fieldhouse, B.A. excused himself to the nun and went down to the end of the hallway, where the main athletic office was located. He rapped his knuckles on the door, then stepped inside. Hannibal was behind the main desk, talking on the phone, while Murdock leafed through an old issue of The Sporting News.

'All right!' Hannibal exclaimed as he hung up the phone. To B.A., he explained, 'That was my agent, Pablo. He says he's onto a hot new lead and wants to run it past me over dinner. From the sound of it, I might be able to hang up my Aquamaniac outfit for good if it comes through. Ain't that great?'

'Pablo's a flake,' B.A. responded cynically. 'Man wears

two hundred dollar shoes with no socks. . .'

'All agents are flakes,' Hannibal said with a shrug. 'It goes with the job. Where's Face? I wanna have a chance to spiff up. Pablo's even footing the bill for this one. . .at the Polo Lounge, no less. . .'

'He had to talk somethin' over with Billy,' B.A. said.

Murdock set down his magazine and moved over to B.A. 'You inspire men, B.A.. You are a natural leader. I stand in awe of the Baracian One!'

'You still on that kick, fool?' B.A. taunted. 'Give it a rest, Murdock. I got no time for jibber-jabber.'

Murdock looked back at Hannibal, a loopy grin on his face. '"Got no time for jibber-jabber." It's even got poetic metre, Hannibal, I swear it. Iambic pentameter. My God, the man speaks in verse!'

'What's he blabbin' about now?' B.A. asked Hannibal. 'Man, last time I talked in verse was when I got some of that crazy man's blood from a transfusion!'

'Never mind, B.A.,' Hannibal said, getting up from behind the desk. 'Let's just get a move on, can we? I don't want to have to keep Pablo waiting.'

The door of the office opened and in walked Face, looking bleak and morose. He sought out the nearest chair and slumped into it, ignoring the others. He seemed lost in a bad dream.

'What gives, Face?' B.A. asked. 'You don't look so good.'

'It's Billy Rey,' Face explained. 'He just told me, out of the blue, that he can't play on Saturday.'

'What do you mean?' Hannibal said. 'Why not?'

'I don't know. I tried to get him to tell me, but he wouldn't say.' Face slowly shook his head. 'If he doesn't play, Banning's gonna bury us so deep in the ground they'll need a geiger counter to find us!'

'It doesn't make any sense,' B.A. said. 'I know we gave him a rough time in practice, but Billy ain't the type to run chicken from a challenge. Something ain't right.'

'You said it,' Face muttered. 'He seems scared all of a sudden, and it's got nothing to do with your dirty defence, B.A. . .'

118

22

Billy Rey had turned sixteen nearly a month ago, and with the acquisition of the rundown Nova, he had gained a certain mobility and, by virtue of his scholastic achievements and record of good conduct, the right to exercise that freedom within the confines of a curfew. As the sun was setting that evening, Billy checked out of his dormitory and slipped furtively through the campus grounds to the parking lot, where he climbed into his Nova and, with some difficulty, started the car and drove off. As he was leaving St Mary's, B.A. pulled his van onto the road behind him. The A-Team had been waiting behind a service shed for the better part of an hour in the hopes that Billy might take off and provide them with a clue as to his sudden withdrawal from the upcoming football game.

'Don't get too close to him, B.A.,' Face said from the front seat as he watched the rear tail-lights of the Nova.

'Hey, this is my ride, man,' B.A. snapped. 'I'll do like I please without any coachin' from you, Coach!'

'It's his ride, Face,' Murdock reiterated from the back of the van. 'Let him do like he pleases.'

'Do I hear an echo here?' Face wondered drolly.

'Hey, the fool's finally making some sense,' B.A. said.

'Yes, oh Baracian One. Yes. You lead and the Murdock will follow.'

'Keep it down, you guys, wouldya?' Hannibal said, cupping his hand over the mouthpiece of the van's mobile phone. He didn't look too pleased with the recent turn of events. 'I'm trying to iron out a delicate situation here, okay?'

'Okay, Hannibal,' Face said, turning his full attention to the Nova. 'Floor's yours.'

Hannibal had been waiting for his agent to be paged at the Polo Lounge, and when Pablo finally got to the phone, Hannibal told him, 'Hey, Pablo. . .*como esta*?'

'Yeah, I'll *como* your *esta*, Smith!' Pablo had a faint Mexican accent, which made it even more difficult for Hannibal to make out what he was saying. 'Where the hell are you?'

'Sorry to call so late, but I'm gonna have to cancel dinner,' Hannibal said. 'Something unexpected came up.'

'That's what I told *you* when we set up this date, gringo,' Pablo complained. 'Hey, I got our names in and I just slipped the maitre d' a fin to get us a decent table! I don't wanna hear no cancellation crap, *comprende*?'

'I really wish I could, Pab, but I just can't get away. Look, how about breakfast tomorrow? On me?'

'Breakfast isn't going to be the only thing that's on you if you don't get down here, pronto! Stand me up on this one, Smith, and you might as well plan on wearin' that rubber creep suit the rest of your career, 'cause I won't be liftin' a finger to help you again. Dig?'

'Pablo. . .c'mon. . .don't be like that.' Hannibal stared daggers at his fellow Team members as he kept trying to soothe his agent's wounded ego. 'Be a sport, *muchacho*, okay? I mean, eating alone isn't the end of life, you know. You'll get a good table and all that visibility. . .who knows, you might lure a real find to come do supper with you.'

'That's a good idea, Smith. With a little luck, maybe I can land somebody to take this part I was gonna hand you on a silver platter. You're a fool, Smith. Grade A meathead.'

'Look, I'm sorry you feel that way, Pablo, but—'

'*Pendejo grande!* That's you, Smith. We're through!'

'Hey, and the same to you,' Hannibal yelled into the receiver. 'Why don't you save my next residual cheque and buy yourself some socks while you're at it!?'

Hannibal slammed the phone down and pulled out a cigar from his pocket, biting off the tip in a fit of anger and spitting it out into the ashtray.

'Didn't go too well, huh?' Murdock guessed.

'What's a *pendejo grande*?'

'I think it's a giant, white-billed duck, Colonel.'

'It's an idiot, man,' B.A. called out from the front seat. 'A moron.'

'Well, he got that right,' Hannibal mused, lighting the cigar. 'I gotta have my head examined; passin' up a chance of a lifetime to go snoopin' on some wayward teenage football star. Is this what we've sunk to, guys?'

'Hey, ease up, Hannibal,' Face said. 'This is legitimate. . . and besides, every member of the Team has the right to call in the other guys when he thinks there's a call for it. I say Billy's got some big problems.'

'Yeah, and he's drivin' one of 'em,' B.A. said. 'Man, he's got so much smoke comin' outta his tailpipes I can barely follow him!'

'I'm serious!' Face insisted. 'Look, while you guys were staking out the parking lot, I started talking to some of the other guys in his dorm, and they all say he's been acting strange the past few days. Breaking curfew on the sly, making a lot of secret phone calls when he thinks everyone's asleep. Good as he's been playing, the kids say he's still way off his game. He's in trouble, and he needs our help. . .'

'What do you want from me?' Hannibal chided. 'A signed affidavit? Take a good look, the *pendejo grande* is here. . .and Pablo is at the Polo Lounge, glaring at a plate of steamed clams thinking up some new names to call me.'

Murdock tried to put down the dissension with a display of cheerleading that would have put a pep rally to shame. 'Hey, guys, I just love it when we take off together on a case, don't you? I just love that rush of adrenalin. . .the sense of forward motion. . .the sense of the lurking unknown out there. . .lurking. Oh, man, there's nothing like it, nothing in the world! Don't you agree, B.A.? Hey, how about some inspiring words from the Baracian One?'

B.A. eyed Murdock in the rear-view mirror and curled his upper lip just enough to let a long, loud growl spill out into the van.

'Brief, but full of inspiration,' Murdock declared, undaunted by B.A.'s strained temper.

As they continued to follow Billy from a distance, the chase wound its way slowly into the more destitute part of the city. Groomed suburban lawns gave way to asphalt playgrounds surrounded by crumbling tenements. Winos and transients wandered the sidewalks, trying to stay clear of the dim illumination cast by the few streetlights that hadn't been shot out with pellet guns or slingshots. A few blocks over, a lone siren wailed through the growing darkness, on its way to or from some nightly altercation that had resulted in a call to the police.

'Hey, these are some mean streets,' B.A. observed, turning a corner to keep up with the Chevy. 'I spent some time here when I was a kid, and I couldn't wait to get outta here. Man, I enlisted and went to Nam 'cause it was my only ticket out!'

'I wonder what Billy's doing here?' Face murmured.

'Definitely not joyriding,' Hannibal said. 'I think we're gonna find out real soon what's been bugging him.'

Sure enough, a few blocks later, Billy pulled to a stop in front of a ramshackle apartment complex and turned off his engine. He waited a moment, then got out of the car and bounded up the littered steps and into the building. B.A. slowly drove past, then pulled into a parking spot down the street.

'Okay, how we gonna handle this?'

For all his initial reluctance, Hannibal was now on top of the situation, sensing that a good dose of the jazz was in the making. He quickly took charge.

'Face, go on in.' Hannibal handed him a walkie-talkie.

'Take this. I'll be behind you on a count of thirty.'

'Fair enough.' Face opened the door and slipped out into the street, waiting for a car to pass before bounding across to the tenement and up the steps that had led Billy out of sight.

'Murdock, cover the vehicle,' Hannibal ordered on his way out of the van. 'B.A. you're in charge of the street.'

'Right,' B.A. said.

'Affirmative,' Murdock said, taking another walkie-talkie and handing a third to B.A.

As the three men moved out into their respective positions, they were being watched by Mike and Ryack, who had been in the car that passed Face moments earlier. From their parking space at the corner, Ryack monitored the A-Team's movements as he spoke into a car phone. 'I don't know who they are,' he said. 'Four guys in a van. . .I might be wrong, but I think maybe they might be Billy Rey's football coaches. Whoever they are, we're gonna need some backup. . .good, good. We're at sixteen hundred and fifty-seventh street.'

Ryack hung up the phone, then pulled out a revolver from under the dashboard. Mike already had his gun out.

'Should we check 'em out, Ryack?'

'Yeah,' Ryack said, quietly opening his door and unsnapping the safety on his revolver.

23

Face followed the young quarterback up three flights of steps, then sought refuge in a cramped alcove while Billy paused outside a third floor apartment and rapped on the door. The corridor was dimly lit and wallpaper was flaking in more places than it held together, but the faded carpet showed signs of recent sweeping and there was a faint odour of disinfectant testifying to attempts by some of the tenants to stave off the deterioration of the building.

When the apartment door opened, a black woman in her late twenties gasped at the sight of Billy, then rushed out to embrace him. In her spiked heels, she was a few inches taller than the youth. 'Billy! Thank God you're okay!'

Billy returned her hug, then broke away from the woman and told her, 'Charlotte, you can't stay here. You've gotta go someplace where they can't get to you.'

Charlotte set her slender hands on her hips. 'All of us have agreed we're not going to work for that man again, no matter what,' she declared. 'It's over.'

'That's good, but I still gotta get you outta here,' Billy said, looking past Charlotte into the apartment, where an older woman stared out apprehensively from behind an ironing board heaped high with wrinkled clothes. 'Where are the others?'

'They're coming tonight from Vegas. By car.'

'We'll tend to them later, then. Is your stuff packed?'

Charlotte picked up an overnight bag from a chair near the door. 'I don't have much. . .'

'Let's go!' Billy turned to the woman by the ironing board. 'Thanks for letting Charlotte wait here, Mrs Fuller. You've been a big help.'

'Be careful,' the woman responded. 'Hoodlums play for keeps and I don't want to see either of you hurt.'

Face had been able to pick up scraps of conversation, but he couldn't figure out what was happening, although the mention of hoodlums put him on his guard. When Billy and Charlotte started down the hallway toward him, Face quickly slipped out the window behind him and found himself on a fire escape riveted to the side of the tenement. The flimsy structure creaked slightly when he moved, so he stayed put momentarily and looked down to the street. From his position, he had a clear view down the street, and when he saw a handful of men pile out of a dark sedan to join Ryack and Mike at the corner, Face brought his walkie-talkie to his lips and whispered, 'Six new players, B.A., Murdock. A black sedan half a block up from the van. They're on foot now, comin' your way. I think I see some iron on 'em, so watch out.'

'Got 'em,' B.A.'s voice crackled over the small speaker.

As he was clipping the walkie-talkie back to his waist, Face heard a noise directly below him. Adrenalin shot through him and he was ready to dive back inside the building when he saw that it was Hannibal, who had just climbed out onto the fire escape from the second floor. Face gathered his wits and was going to climb down to join him when Hannibal called up to him on the walkie-talkie.

'Hold your ground, Face.'

Face brought the walkie-talkie back to his mouth. 'Hannibal, what's the plan?'

'I think we ought to hold back and see what happens. Be ready to fire in case it comes down to that. You got a good cover position up there?'

'Yeah, I can manage,' Face said, crouching down on the

fire escape landing. 'Hey, there's Billy now, with some woman he picked up in the apartment.'

'Okay, everybody brace themselves,' Hannibal told the Team as he took the safety off his gun. 'Be ready for anything.'

As they left the building, both Billy and Charlotte scanned the street nervously before hurrying to the waiting Nova, passing the spot where B.A. was hiding.

'Hannibal,' B.A. hissed into his walkie-talkie once he had a clear view of the woman. 'That girl looks like Charlotte King to me.'

'Charlotte King?' Face muttered from the fire escape. The name clearly didn't register with him.

'Charlotte King, Charlotte King.' From his hiding place behind the van, Murdock recited the name like a mantra. It didn't bring him to nirvana, however. 'Who's Charlotte King?'

'The lead singer for the Bells?' Hannibal conjectured from his second-story perch.

'Yeah, it's her, all right,' B.A. said. 'And she's about to have company from some dudes who don't look like fans. . .'

.Ryack led the reception committee that descended upon the Nova like Earl Schieb salesmen working on commission. Billy and Charlotte stopped a few feet from the car when they saw the hardware pointing their way.

'Miss King,' Ryack spoke with mock politeness, 'you and your half-brother are comin' with us. Our wheels are a little classier than this bolt heap.'

'You're one of Carlin's men,' Charlotte guessed. 'Leave us alone!'

'Now, you know we can't do that.' Ryack waved his arm and one of the sedans down the block lurched forward, approaching the group. 'Don't make any more problems for yourselves. We don't wanna have to wake up the neighbourhood, do we?'

As the sedan was halfway to its destination, a burst of gunfire from the tenement fire escape took out the car's front wheels, sending Ryack's men dashing for cover as the screeching vehicle raced out of control into their midst. Ryack and Mike seized Charlotte and Billy and began dragging them down the street toward the other sedan.

B.A. barely managed to roll away from a stack of garbage cans before the runaway car tumbled over the curb and sent trash flying as it flipped upside down, rattling its occupants to the point where they were unable to do much but lie still, groan and hope their rash of aches were due to bruises and not broken bones.

Murdock was already in the van by the time B.A. got behind the wheel and started the engine.

'Excellent gymnastics back there, oh Baracian One,' Murdock exclaimed over the gun blasts he fired at the thugs who had scattered to various nooks and begun firing at Face and Hannibal on the fire escape.

'Shut up and hold tight, Murdock!' B.A.'s biceps bulged as he jockeyed the van out into the street and raced to intercept Ryack and Mike, who were within a dozen yards of the second sedan.

Billy lent some quick assistance to the proceedings when he pretended to trip on a manhole cover and fell forward. In the same motion, he grabbed Mike's wrist and jerked the criminal sharply forward so that he slammed into Ryack, who lost his grip on Charlotte. With his well-trained reflexes, Billy was able to recover his balance and throw a tackle on the two men, bringing them to the asphalt.

'Run for it!' he shouted to Charlotte over his shoulder.

'Not without you!' She helped Billy to his feet, then kicked off her heels so the two of them could flee faster. Unaware of who was in the approaching van, they ran in the opposite direction, heading back toward the apartment building. B.A. rolled down his window and tried to call out to Billy, but the resounding gunfire throughout the neighbourhood was too loud.

'Reverse, B.A.!' Murdock said as he winged a would-be assailant with a well-placed shot, then crawled into the back of the van and headed for the rear doors.

By now Face had joined Hannibal on the second storey

level of the fire escape, and bullets chewed at the brickwork and steel framework around them as they traded shots with the gunmen down on the street. Fortunately, Ryack's men were too busy trying to pick off Hannibal and Face to pay much attention to Billy and Charlotte.

'I gotta get to 'em before they go back in,' Hannibal told Face. 'Cover for me. . .'

Hannibal gave his gun to Face, then raced out to the end of the fire escape, letting his weight swing the ladder down to the alley. He jumped off before the ladder clanged against the asphalt, then staggered forward, catching Billy and Charlotte as they rushed up onto the sidewalk.

'It's okay,' Hannibal assured them. Once he was sure Billy had had a chance to recognise him in the dim light, Hannibal pointed to the van which was screeching backwards towards them, its rear doors opening to reveal Murdock fanning his pistol at a few pesky hoods trying to blow out the van's tyres. 'Come on, that's our ticket outta here!'

B.A. brought the van to a quick halt at the entrance to the alley, giving Hannibal time to usher Billy and Charlotte into the back. Murdock leaned up and unlocked the ceiling hatch, then looked up through the opening and called out to Face, 'Last call for passengers!'

As B.A. put the van into first and squealed out of the alley, Face climbed over the railing and pushed off, timing his jump so that he landed with all fours on the van's roof. Bullets whistled above his head as he flattened himself against the roof and held on for dear life as B.A. floored the accelerator and raced down the street.

'Who are you?' Charlotte gasped once she was able to find her voice in the wake of the excitement.

'They're my football coaches,' Billy explained, himself bewildered by the events of the past few minutes.

'I think you may need more than a coach, Miss King,' Hannibal said as the sound of gunfire faded outside the van. 'Allow me to introduce myself. I'm Hannibal Smith, and this is The A-Team.'

'The A-Team?' Billy said, stunned. As Face crawled in through the hatch and grinned at the quarterback, Billy shook his head with amazement. 'Man, this is hot!'

'Now that we've all had enough fun and games for one night,' Hannibal told his guests, 'maybe you'd be kind enough to let us know what's going on around here. . .?'

24

Charlotte wanted to hold off on explanations until she was sure that her friends had safely arrived from Las Vegas. As Hannibal had rightly guessed, Charlotte was lead singer of the highly successful singing group The Bells, and the friends she spoke of were the three women who sang back-up vocals on the gold album that had recently catapulted them to stardom. According to plans made during a hasty long-distance phone call earlier that day, Charlotte was to meet with the other women at a small warehouse located near the train yards in Glassell Park, on the other side of the freeway from Elysian Park and Dodger Stadium. During the lean, early years of the Bells' career, they had used the warehouse for rehearsals, learning to stretch their voices while trying to sing over the rattling of the trains that rolled through the yards at all hours.

Shortly after ten, while a fifty-car train from Bakersfield lumbered through the yard enroute to San Pedro, a cherry red Cadillac pulled off San Fernando Road and rolled to a stop in front of the warehouse doors. The headlights flashed on and off three times in quick succession. Moments later, the warehouse door groaned open and the Cadillac inched its way into the black gloom within. Behind the wheel was Jennifer Kim, a dark-haired

Oriental woman dressed in gleaming satin. Beside her was Marcia Clifford, whose frosted hair sharply contrasted with the darkness of her skin and the dyed leather of her outfit. Lilianna Ramirez sat in the back seat, nervously running her fingers through the henna ringlets that cascaded from her head. As Jennifer turned off the engine, the three women sat in uneasy silence, peering out into the darkened enclosure.

'I don't like this,' Marcia whispered. 'Where is she?'

Lilianna let out a sudden, involuntary shriek when an overhead light flashed on and she saw B.A. standing by the light switch with Templeton Peck. Although the warehouse door was closing behind the Cadillac, Jennifer reflexively reached for the ignition, fearing that she'd blundered into a trap.

'It's okay, girls,' Face called out. 'We're with Charlotte. It's okay. . .honest.'

The women kept the Cadillac's windows rolled up and the doors locked as the two men approached them. 'Where is Charlotte?' Marcia asked through the glass. 'Why did she say to come here instead of her hotel? On the phone she sounded—'

'Whoah, whoah, one question at a time,' B.A. said. 'You ladies are in trouble and we're here to help. That's all you gotta know right now.'

In the back seat, Lilianna was eyeing Face with a strange expression on her face. She finally rolled her window down a crack and asked him, 'Don't I know you? From the orphanage?'

Face nodded. 'I think so. You're Lilianna, right? Youngest cheerleader for the football team the last year I was at St Barth's?'

Lilianna nodded. 'Now it's St Mary's.'

'I know,' Face said.

Lilianna told Marcia and Jennifer, 'It's okay. This is Templeton Peck. He was a big sports hero at the orphanage before you two showed up.'

B.A. shook his head with disbelief. 'You mean all you girls come from the same orphanage?'

'Along with Charlotte,' Face reminded him. 'We've got a reunion here.'

When the women unlocked their doors, Face and B.A. opened them. As Lilianna got out, she searched the shadows. 'Where's Charlotte?'

'Right here,' Charlotte said, coming in through a side door with Hannibal and Murdock. She broke away from the men and joined her girlfriends for an emotional greeting. 'It's so good to see you got here. I was worried to death!'

'Why? What's going on?' Jennifer enquired. 'Is it something to do with the contracts?'

As Charlotte was quickly explaining her recent scrape with Ryack and the other thugs, Hannibal pointed to the Cadillac and told B.A., 'Sweep it, big guy.'

B.A. nodded, taking the debugging device in his hand and waving it slowly before him as he began circling the car.

'What are you doing?' Marcia asked him.

'Lookin' for bugs,' B.A. said.

Hannibal explained further, 'We're just taking some needed precautions. Charlotte tells us you girls are having some trouble with your record company. As luck would have it, trouble is our main source of employment, not to mention satisfaction.'

'Hannibal, we got another one.' B.A. reached under the rear bumper of the Cadillac and unfastened a transmitter similar to the one that had been placed on Billy Rey's Nova.

'Okay, we gotta act fast here.' As Hannibal raised the door through which the Cadillac had entered the warehouse, he told B.A., 'You and Murdock go park this baby somewhere else. Put the bug back on so we can throw 'em off the scent, then hustle back here. Face, go help Billy on look-out while I run the ladies through a briefing and find out what we're up against.'

As the rest of the Team headed off to undertake their various duties, Hannibal herded The Bells into the back office of the warehouse. He pulled the shades and set a lamp close to the floor behind a desk to keep the light down to a minimum. As the women took seats around him, he stationed himself near the door, where he could see most of the warehouse area through a crack in the shade.

'Someone was following us down from Vegas?' Lilianna wondered. 'Is that what that bug was all about?'

'That's right, and as near as we can guess, the culprits have to be some heavies working for your record company. Charlotte says you're refusing to resign a new contract with them and that you've all been getting a lot of threats since then, right?'

Marcia nodded. 'Those creeps skim off ninety percent of what we make. It's like a slave contract. We were tricked into signing it, thinking that the ninety percent was supposed to be ours, but the wording was juggled to make it end up being the other way around.'

'And what's the name of the company?' Hannibal said.

'Black Label,' Charlotte divulged. 'Carlin Black Label, to be exact. . .a little pun on the beer, I guess.'

'Carlin?' Hannibal said. 'Did you say Carlin?'

'Yes,' Charlotte said. 'That's right. He's big, fat, mean, and as low as they come, if you ask me.'

'Well, it certainly is a small world,' Hannibal reflected wryly. 'We just met the man a few days ago in Miami. Seems that in addition to running a record company he's also got his fingers into gambling interests, real estate scams and who knows what else. . .'

'Yes, that's the same man!' Lilianna exclaimed. 'His main offices are in Chicago. He was supposed to fly out to Vegas to try to renegotiate our contracts, but he said some pressing business came up in Florida and he'd have to postpone. That's when we decided to go ahead and just break things off with his company. I mean, we just had a gold record and all we have to show for it is a nice wardrobe and one Cadillac for the four of us to share! It isn't right!'

'We're going to have to do something about that,' Hannibal said. 'Carlin was able to avoid getting thrown in the slammer when we shut down his operations in Miami, but now that we've got another chance at him, things should be interesting. . .shhhhh. Someone's coming. . .'

There was silence in the office as Hannibal readied his pistol and peered out at the warehouse. The side door had creaked open, and two men slipped inside. Hannibal let out a breath and relaxed.

'It's okay, they're with us.'

B.A. and Murdock crossed the deserted enclosure to the office. Hannibal let them in.

'I dumped the Caddy on the other side of the freeway, near one of them lots for Dodger fans,' B.A. reported. 'If those goons track it down, they'll think the girls went to the ballgame. . .'

'Good thinking, B.A.,' Hannibal said. 'Now I think it'd be a good idea if we made ourselves scarce, just in case somebody's done their homework and knows about this place.'

The group stealthily left the warehouse and met up with Face and Billy on the way to the van, which was parked behind another of the buildings. Hannibal filled the rest of the team in on the identity of their adversary, and it was quickly decided that butting heads with Carlin again was just the sort of thing everyone needed to get back in shape after the long lay-off from plying their mercenary trade.

As B.A. drove onto the freeway, heading back to the Valley and The A-Team's Encino hideaway, the other men got down to discussing strategy.

'I think we should let these ladies hole out in the Valley while we take care of business,' Face said.

'Take Care of Business!' Murdock piped in. 'Yes, that's a definite plan, there, straight from the planbook of the Baracian One. That's what we should do, all right!'

'Thanks, Murdock,' Face said, 'I'm glad we have your blessing.'

'Okay, then that's settled,' Hannibal said, telling the women, 'It's a nice place. You can just hang low for the weekend. We shouldn't need much more time than that to work—'

'But we can't!' Charlotte protested. 'We promised to sing at a benefit for a children's hospital here in LA. It's a charity we've supported since we first started out. Carlin's always thrown fits because he doesn't make any money from it.'

'That's another reason why we broke off the contract when we did,' Lilianna went on. 'He tried to stipulate that if we did any charity shows, he would take a cut out of our regular earnings to compensate for what he wouldn't be making otherwise. Worse than that, he said if we kept insisting on doing gigs for free, we might find ourselves becoming suddenly accident-prone.'

'Where's this concert supposed to be?' Hannibal asked.

'At the Greek Theatre,' Charlotte told him. 'Saturday night.'

'The Greek?' Face gasped. 'Saturday night? We can't cover you there. You'll have to cancel, that's all there is to it!'

'Hey, it's for *children*, Face!' B.A. said from the front seat.

'Come on, Face,' Murdock sniffed. 'You heard the Baracian One. Get a little guts. Step up and be counted. Are you a man or a mouseketeer?'

Face sighed and looked out the window at the streaming traffic around them. 'Terrific. I really love this, Murdock.'

'Knock it off, you guys.' Hannibal began toying with one of his cigars as he brainstormed, then said, 'If I know Carlin, he'll be on his way here to make sure this little problem of his doesn't get any more out of hand. Charlotte, can you think of any place he'd hang out in LA?'

'Sure. He's got a penthouse office on Sunset. That's where he wined and dined us before we made the mistake of signing on with him.'

'Good, then we'll start there.'

Jennifer asked, 'What are you going to do?'

Hannibal clipped the end off his cigar, then set it in his mouth and applied a match to it. As he puffed away contentedly, he said, 'I think the Bells need a personal manager. . .someone with vision. . .someone who can see into the future and plot your careers with style and wisdom.'

'Who might that be?' Charlotte wondered.

'Yours truly,' Hannibal said. 'Call me Danny Diamond, Agent and Personal Manager to the stars. Mr Peck will draw up the appropriate papers. Pablo, ol' buddy, watch out. . .'

25

This just wasn't Charles Carlin's month.

First there had been the problems in Miami Beach. With the demolition of his planned hotel and the imprisonment of Joey Epic and his ragtag band of followers, Carlin was forced to stay in Florida for the better part of a week, working in conjunction with his coterie of crack lawyers and the Cardenac Brothers to make sure that he could salvage some sort of influence in the resort city and lay the groundwork for a new master plan that might eventually provide the sort of pay-off he was looking for. As if that dilemma hadn't been enough to try his patience, he had returned to Chicago and found his office cluttered with telegrams advising him that the Bells were bailing out of their contract with his record company back out west, thus threatening still another of his bigger sources of income. Subscribing to the maxim that if he wanted anything done right he would have to do it himself, Carlin had booked the next flight out of O'Hare and arrived in Los Angeles the morning after the botched abduction of Charlotte King and Billey Rey. Showing up at the Black Label penthouse offices on Sunset Boulevard, Carlin had closed himself off in the executive office with Teddy Ryack to get the full details of the previous evening's fiasco. Upon hearing the description of the men who had thwarted the would-be kidnapping, Carlin began to quake like clothed jello.

'Them again!' he seethed, pounding a meaty fist on the desktop in front of him. 'Who are they? Fast Tony's boys? I don't believe this!'

'I don't think they're with Tony,' Ryack ventured, rubbing a visible bruise on his cheek received during the scuffle in the ghetto. 'My guess is they aren't workin' for anybody but themselves. They're tough, whoever they are.'

'Hey, tell me about it!' Carlin swung his chair around and stared a moment out the picture window overlooking Sunset. A large billboard touting the upcoming benefit concert by the Bells at the Greek Theatre taunted him from atop a record store across the street. Turning back to Ryack, he asked, 'And what about the rest of the group? You had 'em followed from Vegas with a bug on their Cadillac, didn't you?'

Ryack fidgeted in his seat. From the look of misery on his face, it almost seemed as if he were contemplating a swan dive through the penthouse window rather than having to own up to yet another failing. 'John was about five miles behind 'em all the way down,' he finally said, 'but when he caught up with the Caddy, it had been ditched in a lot near Dodger Stadium. We sat on it all night, but they didn't come back.'

'So we lost the whole damn group,' Carlin concluded. 'I have a dozen studio musicians down in Studio Six, bleeding me by the minute waitin' to lay down tracks on the new album. I got a pressing company on hold and yippin' for product. We have release schedules already more fouled up than any I've had to deal with since I formed this joint. . .and you lose the whole group.'

'Sorry, Mr Carlin.'

'"Sorry Mr Carlin." "We couldn't help it, Mr Carlin." "Those guys sure are tough, Mr Carlin."' The fat mogul pried himself out of his chair and leaned across the desk, pointing a thick finger at Ryack. 'Maybe I oughta cut a record with you and Joey Epic whinin' and makin' excuses for screwin' things up all the time. You'd make a hell of a duo the way you sing the same lines over and over again. . .'

Carlin's tirade was interrupted by the buzzing of the office phone. He grabbed the receiver and nearly bit off the mouthpiece in his anger. 'Yeah, what is it, Grace?'

'It's Mel, in Studio Six. Apparently there's a man down there who says he's the new personal manager for The Bells.'

'Oh, is that a fact?' Carlin's eyebrows danced at the news. 'Okay, thanks, Grace.'

As Carlin hung up the phone, Ryack asked him, 'Good news?'

'Could be. Look, if you wanna get outta the doghouse, why don't you get together a few of your best men and meet me at Studio Six. I have a hunch there's going to be a pest there in need of exterminating. . .'

Ryack got out of his chair and told Carlin, 'You can count on me, boss.'

'If you mess up again, Ryack, you're gonna end up in so many pieces that I'll need a calculator to count 'em!'

Once the flunky had left his office, Carlin removed a small key from his vest pocket and unlocked a desk drawer. Inside, amidst a stack of important papers, was a palm-sized derringer. Carlin checked to make sure it was loaded, then slipped the gun in his coat pocket as he headed out into the hallway. Reaching the elevators, he rode down to the sixth floor, then stepped out and proceeded to the recording studio.

Hannibal and Face were parading around the facilities in fancy three-piece suits, wearing almost enough gold between them to give B.A. a run for the money. Hannibal, dressed in white, toted a silver-headed cane, while Face carried a leather-tooled briefcase. Hannibal paused in front of a stand and eyed the sheet music posted there, then shook his head angrily at Mel, an emaciated man in his thirties with slicked-back hair and an outfit that looked as if it had been borrowed from a costume shop specialising in The Old West Look.

'These arrangements were done without my consent,'

139

Hannibal sniffed contemptuously, flipping through the pages of sheet music and tossing them over his shoulder like failed jokes in a Johnny Carson monologue. 'I gotta nix this one, and this one, and this one. And what in the world is this? Please, not a song with doo-ahhs. Can you believe this, Lonnie?' he asked Face, 'They got the Bells singing doo-ahhs, for cryin' out loud!'

'Preposterous,' Face snorted, drumming his fingers against the side of his briefcase.

'Look, I don't know who you clowns are,' Mel said, hitching up his faded Levis, 'But I got musicians comin' in here shortly to lay down some tracks, and if you know what's good for you, you'll take your show on the road and get outta here before I have to call security.'

'Let me take care of 'em, Mel,' Carlin said as he emerged from the sound booth and eyed Hannibal and Face.

'Well, long time no see, Chuckie poo,' Hannibal told the overweight mobster. 'Nice tan you picked up in Miami, I see.'

Carlin's skin was pale, although he became a little red around the neck and temples as he waded through the music stands to confront his antagonisers. 'I got a contract out on you guys. How nice of you to drop by and save me the trouble of having you tracked down.'

'Speaking of contracts,' Hannibal said, 'How about if we dispense with the chit-chat and get down to business. My name's Danny Diamond. . .Diamond Management. Besides tying your hired help into knots, we also like to dabble in the arts. I trust somebody's told you we're taking over the reins with The Bells.'

'So you say.'

'Lonnie,' Hannibal asked Face, 'show this carnivorous jackass our contract.'

'Gladly.' Face set his briefcase on a stool and snapped open a side compartment. He pulled out a file and handed it to Carlin. 'We have been commissioned by The Bells to act in their behalf. You will see that these documents have been notarised and executed consistent with the legal

140

procedures of the State of California, et cetera and so forth. . .'

'This should be good for a laugh,' Carlin murmured as he donned a pair of glasses to read over the contracts. 'Hmm, you guys sure know how to sling around the legal mumbo jumbo, I'll grant you that. Too bad it isn't worth the paper it's written on.'

'So you say,' Hannibal mocked.

Face leaned forward and pointed out a section of the contract to Carlin. 'You'll note that it gives us full power of attorney over all decisions for The Bells. Not restricted to, but including wardrobe, selection of songs, publicity, ad infinitum, et cetera and so forth. . .'

'Well, I'll be sure to file these in an important place,' Carlin said as he ripped up the contracts and dropped them in a nearby wastebasket. When he turned back to Hannibal and Face, he had his derringer out. 'Now then. . .you've had your fun, but I fear that all good things must come to an end. I want The Bells back here in this studio in an hour or else you'll be taking your meals through a tube.'

'You're going to have to come up with better help than you've had in the past,' Hannibal advised Carlin, paying no attention to the derringer. 'Why don't you put that toy away? Also, since you tossed out that contract before you had a chance to read it all, I suppose I should tell you our copies confirm that all profits due The Bells for their last album and tour are going to be transferred to a Diamond Management account for redistribution.'

'Is that all?' Carlin kept his gun out, but held back from using it. 'And when is all this supposed to happen?'

'What time is it now, Lonnie?'

Face checked his watch. 'Nine twenty-six.'

'I don't like to be pushy,' Hannibal said. 'so why don't we say that this agreement goes into effect at nine twenty-seven sharp, Carlin. That gives you thirty or forty seconds to wipe the spit off your chin and stop breathing through your mouth.'

'You got a real case of the cutes, my friend.' Carlin

waved his derringer slightly. 'This might be a small gun, but it does the job. You, Diamond. . .tell me where The Bells are hiding out or I'm going to give your lawyer a few new button holes on his suitcoat.'

Hannibal grinned over at Face, telling him, 'Well, Lonnie, I think the double-breasted look's coming back into vogue anyway, don't you?'

'Maybe.' Face looked at Carlin and said, 'Look, I appreciate the offer, but I already have a tailor.'

The door behind Hannibal opened and Ryack stepped into the studio, gun drawn. Behind him were three other armed men.

'Frisk 'em!' Carlin ordered. As the men moved in on Hannibal and Face, the chieftain taunted, 'Nice try, gents, but this is a high-pressure business, and when you lose, you lose big. You should have quit back in Miami Beach when you were ahead.'

Hannibal raised his cane at an awkward angle, and just as Ryack was about to search him for weapons, a shotgun blast charged out from the cane's tip, nearly blowing away the hoodlum's feet. As it was, Ryack leapt frantically to one side, bowling over the men behind him. Hannibal lashed out with his cane, striking Carlin's hand and sending the derringer flying. Mel scurried for cover behind a drum kit as Face reached into his briefcase and came out with an Uzi submachine gun, which he used to perforate the ceiling above the heads of Carlin's men. Unwilling to pit their handguns against Hannibal's cane and the Uzi, Ryack and the others dropped their weapons and raised their arms in the air. In a matter of mere seconds, the tables had been turned on Carlin and he found himself the target of someone else's aimed revolver.

'Yes, this certainly is a high-pressure industry,' Hannibal conceded. 'But, as we like to say at Diamond Management, "Pressure makes diamonds."'

'Et cetera and so forth,' Face put in, gathering the fallen guns into his briefcase on his way to the door. Hannibal joined him, pausing in the doorway long enough to leave Carlin with a few words of wisdom.

'Our business is concluded for the moment, Carlin. If you're smart, you'll cut your losses and butt out of The Bells' affairs from here on in. Make any more trouble for us and we'll put you in the obituaries. . .'

26

'I think that went very well, don't you, Face?' Hannibal cracked as he and Peck bounded down the stairwell, clearing two and three steps at a time in their haste to reach the ground floor unmolested by Carlin's security force.

'Don't be on the jazz, Hannibal,' Face pleaded between breaths as he saw the manic gleam in his partner's eyes. 'Please. We're not outta this place yet, you know.'

'Details, details.' Hannibal grabbed the railing as he reached the next landing and swung himself around with the brunt of his momentum, gaining another second.

'"Pressure makes diamonds." Where did that come from?'

'Creative impulse,' Hannibal boasted. 'Sometimes I amaze even me.'

The rousing din of an alarm system suddenly jangled to life in the stairwell and as Hannibal and Face reached the third floor landing, the door to the hallway swung open and two burly men rolled out. One of them caught Hannibal off guard and pinned him to the railing while the other followed up with a hearty right cross to the stomach that quickly reminded Hannibal how tender his ribs were.

'Aren't you boys forgetting something?' Face cried out as he threw himself back up the steps, lashing out with a

144

judo chop and stiff-legged kick. Each blow hit its mark, and while one of Carlin's men tumbled down the steps, the other reeled backwards, knocking himself out when his head collided with the unyielding slats of the panelled stairway wall. Hurrying over to Hannibal, Face extended a hand to his fallen comrade. 'Upsy-daisy. . .how're those ribs?'

'It only hurts when I don't laugh,' Hannibal groaned, regaining his feet. As they resumed their flight, he told Face, 'Thanks for the hand. I didn't know you cared.'

'It's that cologne, Colonel. When you wear it, it drives me wild.'

'What cologne?' Hannibal said, reaching to his shirt pocket and removing a pair of broken cigars whose aroma was seeping through ripped cellophane. 'Look what got in the way of somebody's fist. Remind me to add these onto Carlin's bill.'

They managed to make it outside of the building without further incident, but the moment they started to cross the parking lot, Hannibal and Face spotted three more men taking up the chase.

'Where does he get all that beef?' Hannibal wondered as he took one of the guns from Face's briefcase and used it to send the pursuers ducking for cover behind several limos and sports cars parked near the side of the building. Face pulled out the walkie-talkie and quickly passed along a message.

'Three bogies on the east side of the lot, B.A., and they're armed, so watch it!'

'You got it!'

In a matter of seconds, The A-Team van came crashing through the chain-link fencing into the parking lot and brodied sideways to a halt. B.A. began firing with a handgun while Murdock threw open the rear doors and pumped rounds of hot lead from a fifty-calibre rifle. Hannibal and Face took advantage of the assault to weave their way from car to car toward the van, stopping now and then to trade shots with Carlin's men, who began leaking out of the building at an increased rate.

'They're outnumbering us two to one, oh Baracian One!' Murdock wailed over his shoulder above the sound of his gunfire. 'No, wait, make that three to one. . .now it's more like four—'

'Shut up with the play-by-play, Murdock!' B.A. jammed the gearbox into reverse and backed up to get closer to Hannibal and Face, who were now pinned down by the enemy near a pickup truck. Hannibal emptied the last round from his rigged cane, then covered himself with fire from a handgun as he broke from cover and ran toward the van. Face followed close behind and bullets zipped all around them. One after the other, they leapt headlong into the back of the van, then Murdock pulled the doors shut as B.A. raced out of the parking lot. Several cars screeched out after them, but B.A. quickly lost them in traffic and was soon back on the nearest freeway.

'Well, that was sure fun,' Hannibal said, helping himself to a fresh cigar. 'If we keep making Carlin's men look bad, he'll get rid of 'em for us.'

'Hannibal's on the jazz, guys,' Face warned the others. 'You should have seen him in there. We were staring down the barrels of more guns than someone before a firing squad and he was still grinning like a '55 Buick.'

'What can I say?' Hannibal said, massaging his ribs as he took his first few puffs of the cigar. 'I just love it when—'

'Yeah, yeah, when a plan comes together,' Face grumbled.

Murdock made his way up to the front of the van and slipped into the bucket seat across from B.A., telling him, 'Well done, oh Baracian One. Now what should be our next move? What's going through that big, wonderful head of yours? Command your servants. Lead us. We stand waiting. . .well, actually, we sit waiting, but you know what I mean.'

'What the hell,' Hannibal muttered, 'Go ahead, B.A., call the shots for a change.'

'I think. . .' From the deep furrowing of his brow it was clear that B.A. was doing just that. He kept checking the rear-view mirror as he jockeyed through traffic, watching out for signs of the enemy. 'I think we should head back to the hideout and take a breather before moving on.'

'Oh, wow! What a stupendous idea!' Murdock exclaimed. 'Pure, scintillating genius lurks beneath that noble Mandinka, my friends.'

'How much longer is this going to go on, Murdock?' Face wondered aloud. 'I can't take it much more.'

'Never mind,' Hannibal said. 'It's just a phase. I agree with B.A.. We oughta head back to the Valley. After all, once Carlin quits seein' red he'll go through his waste-basket looking for our phone number on those contracts we drew up. I'll be curious to see what he has to say. . .'

27

Their most recent scrape with danger behind them, it wasn't long before certain immutable laws of nature made themselves known to The A-Team. . .laws that had less to do with life-endangering exploits than the pursuit of overdue pleasures. As B.A. was driving up into the Encino hills, Face approached the subject with all the tact of a comedian at a celebrity roast.

'The only things I like about this case so far are the clients,' he observed. 'Listen, did any of you guys stop to consider that there's four of them, all romantically unattached, and four of us, sharing a similar persuasion?'

'Not only that,' B.A. seconded, 'but there's just enough of them to go around.'

'And not only that,' Murdock joined in, 'but these are inspiring women; women of beauty, verve, wit. . .and they seem to like us, too.'

'Come on, you guys.' Hannibal rubbed his aching ribs as the van bounded over a particularly testy chuckhole. He reminded the others, 'You remember the rule about clients. . .'

'Seems to me we *did* have some kind of silly rule about clients,' Face contemplated. 'What was it? Ahhhhh, now I remember. . ."Be sure to save all receipts and expense vouchers." Isn't that it, Hannibal?'

Hannibal shook his head and tapped ash from the tip of his cigar. 'I know those girls are beautiful and sexy and available, but—'

'Don't forget thrifty, brave, clean and reverent,' Face interjected.

Hannibal ignored the aside and went on, 'But, above all, they're in trouble and they *are* clients. We have a code about messing around with clients. We don't do it. It muddies the atmosphere. It distorts our thinking. It's dangerous. . .'

'Oh yeah, *that* rule,' Face remembered.

'Hannibal's right,' B.A. relented as he pulled into the driveway of their plush hideout. 'We can't mess with these women or we might end up lettin' up on our guard. Of course, once we finish takin' care of business, it'll be another story.'

B.A. stopped the van and the Team climbed out, hearing the sounds of splashing in the backyard pool. Face sighed, 'Well, it seems to me we ought to give ourselves a break here. You know, football players have half-times, basketball players have half-times. . .even baseball players have a seventh-inning stretch, for cryin' out loud. Maybe that's what we need. . .you know, a little breather, a chance to take our minds of more pressing matters. . .'

'Forget it, Face,' Hannibal said. 'It's strictly business, got it?'

Face muttered under his breath as the Team entered the house, only to be startled by the surprised shriek of a woman who sped from the living room like a brown blur before any of the men had a chance to see her.

'Hello?' Face called out. 'Are we interrupting anything?'

'Just a minute,' Charlotte called out from the bathroom, where she'd taken refuge. 'I don't have anything on.'

Face swallowed hard as he traded glances with B.A. 'Strictly business,' he mumbled half-heartedly. 'Strictly business.'

'Steady, Face,' B.A. advised him.

'I'm trying, B.A. I'm trying.'

149

When Charlotte came out of the bathroom, she had a towel wrapped around her and her hair was wet. Smiling awkwardly, she explained. 'I was skinny dipping and left my suit outside.'

'Oh,' Face said. 'How. . .natural.'

Hannibal asked Charlotte. 'The other girls. . .are they presentable out there?' He nodded in the direction of the sliding glass door that led out to the pool area.

Charlotte said, 'Yeah, they're dressed. . .sort of. Go on out. I'll join you as soon as I throw something on.'

'Good idea,' Face said. 'Throw something. . .uh. . .on.'

As Charlotte vanished down a hallway leading to the guest bedrooms, Murdock came up next to Face and confided, 'The trick I've found in these types of situations is to focus the mind on something of a completely different nature. Pick up a copy of Road and Track and look at the cars. . .take eggs from the refrigerator, practice your juggling. Things like that.'

'Easy for you to say,' Face groaned. 'Your mind doesn't focus. Me, I'm in agony here.'

There was no relief to be had when the Team headed out into the backyard. Jennifer was swimming laps in a tight one-piece suit, while Marcia and Kim lay tanning on chaise lounges, the straps to their bikinis untied.

'Hi!' Kim called out to the men. 'Any luck?'

'Luck?' Face said, struggling to keep his eyes from wandering. 'How do you mean?'

'Mr Carlin. You were going to stand up to him. How did it go?'

'Oh, *that*!' As Charlotte joined the group, Face quickly related the highlights of the Team's encounter at the record company, dwelling as much as possible on the dangers they had weathered in the pursuit of their job. The women listened with astonishment, and when Face had finished, Marcia whistled low with amazement.

'I can't believe how fortunate we are to have you guys,' she said as she tied the top of her swimsuit and sat up on the lounge. 'I just wish there was some way we could begin to repay you before you get your hands on our royalties.'

'Well, since we can't get our hands on your *royalties*, then maybe—'

'Face!' Hannibal cut in.

'Never mind,' Face said bleakly. 'We'll just keep a running tab.'

Kim trod water at the deep end of the pool and called out to the Team, 'You could at least join us for a quick swim, couldn't you? The water's fine.'

'I'm sure it is,' Hannibal said, 'but we left Carlin a phone number that's traceable to a hotel in the Valley that we own a stake in. We'll just grab a bite to eat inside, then we have to get a move on. We want to set up a temporary base of operations at the hotel so we don't have to drag you into the dirty work.'

'That's too bad,' Kim said, pushing off from the side of the pool and doing a flawless backstroke through the water. Watching her, Face made a slight whimpering noise in the base of his throat.

'I wonder if there're any eggs in the refrigerator,' he muttered.

'Isn't it a little late for breakfast?' Charlotte asked as she began rubbing sun tan lotion on her bare shoulders.

'I think the Faceman wants to practise his juggling,' Murdock said. 'If there aren't any eggs left, he might have to juggle some issues of Road and Track. . .'

28

The Chestnut Motor Lodge was a small, modest hotel run by a semi-retired couple who had been befriended by The A-Team when their son had been kidnapped by some Vegas mobsters a few years ago. As in similar instances with other clients, the Team had forfeited any upfront payment for their services in exchange for a slice of the hotel's profits and periodic use of the facilities when the need arose. In all, The A-Team had such arrangements with more than a dozen hotels and restaurants in Los Angeles alone, but they had chosen the Chestnut for use in their mission against Charles Carlin because its out-of-the-way location reduced the chances of innocent bystanders being drawn into an altercation. Also, because the hotel's owners had temporarily closed the facilities in order to take a belated second honeymoon in Germany, Hannibal had figured it would be easier to set and spring a trap without having to worry about drawing the attention of other boarders.

When they arrived at the hotel, which was located less than a mile from Dr Kalalau's dental offices in the north end of the Valley, Hannibal went to check on the answer phone to see if Carlin had left any messages. Face began casing out the hotel's perimeters to plot the Team's offence while B.A. and Murdock let themselves into one of the hotel rooms with a clear view of the parking lot and street that ran past the motor lodge. B.A. was carrying a black satchel filled with various tools. Murdock followed close behind him, whispering in the low voice of a golf announcer.

'Baracus is moving to the centre of the carpet. He puts down his satchel. It's a very tense moment here. The fans are hushed, waiting. I don't know, Curt? Do you think he can pull this one off?' Murdock answered himself in another voice from his vast repertoire. 'He's been simply magnificent so far, Chris. All I can say is Baracus has never cracked under pressure. He's steady, he's smooth, and that's what the fans have come to expect.'

Murdock's broadcast ran into some unexpected static when B.A. whirled around and clamped his meaty fingers around his windpipe. 'Why you doin' this, man? Why you doin' jabber jabber all the time in my ear? You're makin' me as crazy as you are!'

Murdock made a choked, gurgling sound until B.A. loosened his grip, then delicately fondled his anguished Adam's apple. 'How long have we known each other, big guy?'

'Too long, sucker,' B.A. said as he bent over to open his satchel.

'Well, I've been watching you in a new light ever since you spared me from the jaws of that menacing Great White, B.A.,' Murdock explained. 'I gotta confess, you're one stupendous, mudsucking wonder. You're a man somebody can admire. I look up to you because of your goodness.'

B.A. glanced over at Murdock, expecting to see a glimmer of sarcasm in his dark eyes. But Murdock was watching him like a lost lamb who'd just caught sight of its shepherd, and in the face of that overwhelming look of sincere admiration even B.A.'s most resolute cynicism fell away from him.

'Oh yeah?' he said, genuinely flattered. 'Well, I do the best I can, you know. I try real hard, you know? I mean, to do what's right. . .y'know?' B.A. was close to choking on his own modesty, and he finally had to look away and busy himself with taking several control boxes and lengths of wiring out of the satchel.

'B.A., you're what's right.' Murdock continued pouring it on as he came over and patted the black man on the back. 'When Howling Mad Murdock is in the fog, you are my fog light and horn. When he's in sub-zero weather, wheels and flaps down, looking for a place to land, you are my navigational system, my runway. You are my air traffic controller.'

'Sheesh, Murdock,' B.A. said, his ears turning red with embarrassment. 'Well, you know, I try to be there for you guys.'

'You do, and you are. And I just want you to know that I'm seeing that, big guy.' Murdock gazed ahead, seeing visions. 'I'm reading that five-by-five. I'm on your wavelength. I'm picking up your signal.'

'I try and talk sense, you know.' B.A. was almost talking to himself now as he tested the toggle switches on the control boxes. 'I try to say what's true. . .cut through all that jibber-jabber.'

'You're the greatest,' Murdock concluded, 'bar none.'

B.A. grinned, baring the gap left by his recently evacuated tooth. 'You're okay, Murdock,' he conceded.

'Together we can change history,' Murdock predicted, his voice filled with messianic fervour. 'Move continents. Part oceans. You have but to command. No job is too difficult!'

'Open that window over there so I can drop the cord out,' B.A. suggested.

'Consider it done, oh Baracian One!' Murdock moved over to the picture window and flipped the latch, then applied his full weight to the frame. It wouldn't budge.

Watching Murdock, B.A. chuckled, 'Man, how we gonna move continents when you can't even open a window?'

'A window does not a continent make,' Murdock claimed.

The door to the hotel room opened and Hannibal walked in, lugging an armload of portable television cameras. 'How's it comin', guys?'

'Give Murdock a hand with that window and we'll be ready to start hookin' things up,' B.A. said, carrying one of the control boxes over to the hotel's TV set, which was locked onto a large metallic stand.

'There was one call on the answer phone,' Hannibal said as he helped Murdock get the window open. 'Nobody said anything but I recognised Carlin's breathing. My guess is we'll have until nightfall to get set up here, then we're gonna have visitors. He's probably put out a call for his best men, so we can't count on having another bunch of creampuffs to blow away.'

'Let them send their stoutest forces!' Murdock cried out. 'Against the prowess of the Baracian One, they will be nothing more than chaff tossed to the wind. It will take more than petty thugs to stand in the way of destiny!'

B.A. set down the control box and went over to pick up one of the cameras Hannibal had set down before helping Murdock. 'Look, Hannibal, I'm sorry about all this gushin' of Murdock's. Don't take any offence. He doesn't know what he's talkin' about.'

'Yeah, sure,' Hannibal said. 'I can handle it.'

'You're still the ace in this deck as far as I'm concerned,' B.A. told him, making sure Murdock couldn't overhear what he was saying. 'I'm just tryin' to humour the guy.'

'Thanks, B.A.,' Hannibal replied. 'I needed that. . .'

29

An old weathered milk truck rolled to a stop down the block from Chestnut Motor Inn shortly after eleven o'clock that night. The six men who slipped out of the truck didn't look like they were in the business of delivering dairy products. Unlike the bicep-laden goods that had come up against The A-Team in recent weeks, these men were of slighter build, dressed in black, with dark, narrow eyes housed in pockets of swarthy flesh. They were all Sicilians, and two of them were identical twins, lethal human bookends differentiated from each other only in that one wore a diamond stud in his left earlobe while the other chose to decorate his right. The Cardenac brothers called their fellow enforcers into a tight huddle near the front of the truck.

'Mr Carlin didn't fly us out here all the way from Miami Beach to disappoint him,' Louis Cardenac reminded everyone. 'There will be no mistakes here tonight. No underestimating the enemy. Antonio?'

Louis's brother took over calling the shots. 'Now, then. . .we have determined that they are in one of the downstairs rooms. Number Eight. You saw it as we drove past. We are going to crush them in a pincer manoeuvre. Vincent, Dom, Joseph, you three take the back way.

Louis and Rico will cover me from the front. I will go in hard and fast. That alone should be enough to take care of things, but if it isn't, I want all of you ready to move in and keep at them until they beg for us to put them out of their misery. Is that clear? Any questions?'

Rico, the oldest member of the group and still years shy of his fortieth birthday, raised a hand and whispered, 'I know Mr Carlin wants these guys alive, but what if they don't want to co-operate?'

Antonio and Louis looked to one another, then bared wicked grins as they withdrew automatic pistols from inside their coats. Antonio proclaimed, 'As far as we're concerned, they didn't give us any choice but to take them out. We go in fast and show them no mercy. Just make sure one of them is kept alive in case Mr Carlin wants to pump them for some information.'

'That's what I wanted to hear!' Rico pulled out his Uzi as well as an ornate switchblade that looked as if it had been passed down through several generations. Joseph, Dom, and Vincent were equally well-armed, and when they broke their huddle and slipped out of sight into various pockets of darkness, it seemed that even the crickets stopped their chirping out of fear that they might incur the wrath of the assassins.

Room Eight was the only unit in the entire hotel with lights on, and the sounds from a blaring TV spilled out through the room's half-opened window. Two silhouettes were visible against the thin material of the curtains, looking like the heads of two people watching the flickering light that emanated from the colour set. Louis and Rico scurried silently to the cover of palm trees that gave them clear shots at the room. Antonio advanced to a point several yards ahead of them, then pulled out a compact walkie-talkie long enough to deliver one final command in a hushed whisper.

'On a five count, hit it with all you've got.'

As he counted off the seconds to himself, Antonio took a deep breath and released the safety on his pistol. Breaking his cover, he rushed the hotel room, and when he'd counted down to zero, he pumped lead into the locks on the front door, demolishing the tumblers so that when he kicked the door it swung inward with minimal resistance. At the same time, the window next to him shattered as a spray of gunfire slammed through both glass and curtains into the figures who had been watching the television. From the other side of the building, the rest of the gang rushed through a back patio area and stormed inside the hotel, making their way down the main hallway to Room Eight. By the time they burst into the room, Antonio Cardenac was already inside, waving his weapon about as he cursed a blue streak of Sicilian curses. To his chagrin, he realised that the room was deserted and that the would-be viewers watching the now-demolished television were nothing more than propped-up pillows that bled foam rubber where they had been pierced by bullets. The A-Team was nowhere to be seen.

'A set-up,' Louis spat angrily as he entered the room. 'We should have figured as much.'

As Rico took out his frustrations on what was left of the television, kicking the set over, Antonio waded through the mess to an end table. He reached for the shade of an overturned lamp and withdrew a small bugging transmitter.

'Whoever you are, congratulations,' he said into the bug.

'You're too kind,' Hannibal's voice came over the built-in speaker next to the bed. 'We accept your compliment. You guys are no slouches yourselves. Sorry we weren't there when you dropped by, but we have this thing about surprise visitors. I hope you understand. Oh, by the way, I like your wardrobe, guys. You almost look like a religious order in those black outfits. You have a funny way of praying, though. . .'

'Where are you!' Rico howled, flashing his switchblade as he looked around the room for hidden cameras. 'Show yourselves and die like men!'

'Now, now, that's hardly an offer we can't refuse,' Hannibal snickered. 'You didn't even say please.'

'Carlin wants you alive,' Louis called out. 'Give up and

we'll see that you get to him that way. Otherwise, you'll find out how the Cardenac brothers earned their reputation.'

'I think we'll take our chances. Life's full of risks,' Hannibal continued to bait the Sicilians. 'I mean, even good pizza can give you indigestion.'

Vincent was searching along one of the walls when he suddenly ripped away a heating duct and pointed inside, telling Antonio, 'Here's their camera!'

'Well done, Vincent.' Antonio raised his gun and aimed it at the camera. 'This conversation is terminated.'

Three more shots rocked the hotel room and the video camera splintered inside the vent. When the reverberation of the gunfire subsided, the Sicilians could hear sirens sounding out in the night, headed their way.

'Let's get out of here,' Antonio hissed at his men. 'We'll see if we can lure them out of hiding.'

30

Hannibal was the only member of The A-Team who had remained inside the hotel during its siege. From his post inside the windowless laundry room, he had monitored the activities of the Sicilians on a series of four mini-screens hitched up to as many cameras, each one situated in a strategic location in and outside the hotel. For protection, he had an AR-15 automatic rifle set across his lap. He watched the Cardenac brothers depart with their fellow killers, having a clear perspective on their movements by way of the remaining three cameras. When it became clear that nobody was headed his way, Hannibal reached to his side for a walkie-talkie and checked in with the rest of the Team.

'They're getting in their truck about now, B.A..'

'We see 'em,' B.A. reported from his post behind the wheel of his van. Murdock sat across from him, watching the milk truck through a pair of binoculars.

'Good,' Hanibal responded. 'Give 'em some space, then start after 'em. Face, you ready on your end?'

Peck was fifty yards down the road, slumped across the front seat of a rental Corvette. Hearing Hannibal over his walkie-talkie, he sat up and fed his key into the car's ignition. 'Affirmative, Hannibal. How about you? Did

160

you manage to stay clear of the fireworks?'

'Yep,' Hannibal said. 'It's sure a good thing we picked the room in the worst need of remodelling, because they sure did a number on it. I'm heading out now, so let's all be ready to trade off on the tail. It should be a lot of fun.'

'I'll say,' Face said, 'I haven't been part of a three-man weave since my old basketball days at St. Barth's.'

In all, The A-Team had rented three vehicles for the evening. Just before B.A. took off in slow pursuit of the passing milk truck, Murdock bounded out of the van and backtracked to a Toyota station wagon parked further down the road. By the time he was inside the auto and revving up the engine, Hannibal was driving past in a late-model BMW.

'Just my luck to get the short straw,' Murdock complained as he pulled out onto the road. 'The Murdock deserved a crack at the Beemer.'

Murdock had forgotten to turn off his walkie-talkie, and Hannibal overheard the complaint, then replied, 'Don't worry, Murdock. Do a good job here and we'll let you go joyriding in the car of your choice the rest of the night.'

'All right!' Murdock slapped on his seat belts and hunched over the wheel. He reached out for his radio, and when he realised he didn't have one, he began singing out loud lyrics from one of his favourite TV shows of all time, *Secret Agent Man*, accompanying himself with his impression of the guitar licks that had backed the original song.

Two racing police cars whipped past B.A. as he was tailing the milk truck, and from the squealing of their sirens he guessed they were headed for the hotel. He was glad no one had put out word yet to block off the area. As it was, he was able to stay close on the track of the fleeing Sicilians, and soon he was able to see the headlights of the other cars lining up behind him, spaced apart by a few hundred feet apiece.

'Okay, I'm ready for the first switch-off,' B.A. said, turning on his blinkers and slowing down. As he rounded the corner, Face eased down on his accelerator and took the van's place behind the milk truck. By the time B.A.

had made a U-turn and headed back to the main road, Hannibal and Murdock had passed, ready to take up lead positions in the chase during the next two trade-offs. It was a complicated strategy in ways, but it served its purpose well, giving the appearance that no one was following the Cardenac brothers.

Inside the milk truck, Rico was peering out the rear windows, gun in hand, and when he saw Murdock's Toyota make a right turn, he turned back to the others. 'There's cars behind us, all right, but nothing's sticking.'

'Damm it all,' Antonio said, keeping his eyes on the road before them. 'If they would have shown themselves, we could have set things right before getting back to Mr Carlin. Now we don't have any choice. It'll only go worse for us if he finds out what happened on the news. . .'

The Sicilians rode on in stony silence, taking little comfort in the realisation that even if they incurred Carlin's wrath, there was little he could do, since none of his men would stand a chance if they tried to take on the Cardenac brothers and their cohorts. Their pride and honour had been tainted by their failure to bring down The A-Team, and, to a man, their sense of shame was every bit as strong as their anger. While they brooded and periodically looked back in the hopes that they would find one tell-tale vehicle following them for a considerable distance, The A-Team continued trading off with one another, all the while hanging back far enough so that it was difficult for those in the milk truck to discern the makes of their vehicles and become suspicious over the continued reappearance of vans, Toyotas, BMWs, and Corvettes.

The chase carried on westward, through the industrial parks of Chatsworth and the suburban housing tracts of Canoga Park, then finally came to a close as the milk truck pulled into a construction site in the foothills of the Santa Susanna Mountains, near Bell Canyon. The wooden framework of designer homes stood out in the moonlight like skeletal remains. A large placard proclaimed this development to be Sunrise Acres, and although the

162

development firm bore the name of Dogburg Enterprises, the real owner of this land parcel and the homes going up on it was none other than Charles Carlin, who had made the purchase primarily with the profits from The Bells' gold album.

Carlin himself was parked near one of the monstrous landmovers, sitting inside a gleaming white Dodge Charger with a rag top. He was eating pistachios out of a bag, tossing the shells in the dirt outside the car. At the sound of the approaching milk truck, Carlin cocked his head to one side and waited for the other vehicle to roll up next to the Charger.

'Well, now,' Carlin said as the Cardenac brothers stepped out of the truck and came over, leaving the rest of the gang inside the truck. 'I take it you have some good news for me.'

'I'm afraid not, sir.' Antonio acted as spokesman. 'They booby-trapped the room and took a powder before we arrived. They're professionals, Mr Carlin—'

'I know they're professionals!' Carlin shouted. 'That's all I've been hearing since they started making my life miserable! That's why I called in you and your boys. I thought you were supposed to be professionals, too.'

'They can't help it if they're outclassed, Carlin,' Hannibal interrupted, popping into view on the other side of the Dodge. He had a gun pointed at Carlin's chest, and behind Hannibal, B.A. aimed a machine gun at the midsection of the Cardenac brothers. To round out the party, Murdock and Face emerged behind the landmover and levelled automatic rifles at the milk truck.

'Tell your "boys" to stay put inside the truck,' B.A. advised the Cardenacs.

As Antonio was relaying the message, Hannibal circled around the front of the Charger and started to get in the driver's side, telling Carlin, 'Slide over and let me have a try behind the wheel here. I thought maybe we'd take a little spin around the property. Who knows, maybe I'll find that little dream house I've been looking for all these years.'

Carlin warily set aside his pistachios and moved to the

passenger's side of the Charger. When B.A. moved into the back seat, Murdock and Face took over guarding the Cardenacs and the other Sicilians.

'Your milkmen made a mess of my office, Chuck,' Hannibal said as he drove up the steady incline leading past rows of unfinished homes. 'I can't say as I liked that. You have a way of doing business that rubs people the wrong way, you know? Take The Bells, for instance. . .'

'Oh, I intend to take The Bells, Mr Diamond,' Carlin declared to Hannibal. 'One way or another, I intend to have them back in my fold.'

'Well, as long as they're in my capable hands, that's not likely to happen.'

'Let's suppose, for the sake of argument, that I was to be willing to take you off the table for a goodly sum of money,' Carlin speculated, softening his tone somewhat. 'You back off this power of attorney nonsense and leave the Bells to me. You'll be happy, I'll be happy—'

'And The Bells would be miserable and exploited,' Hannibal cut in. 'Forget it, I'm not for sale.'

'Well, now, everyone is for sale,' Carlin chuckled. 'It's just the price that's in question.'

'Forget it, man,' B.A. retorted from the back seat. 'Are you deaf, sucker? It ain't gonna happen!!'

'Oh? Not even for a nice round figure. . .something along the line of a cool million tax-free dollars?'

Hannibal pushed in the dashboard lighter and popped a fresh cigar in his mouth. Carlin thought that his offer might be soaking in, but he was mistaken. 'One of the funny things about being just a humble little manager instead of a megabuck operator like yourself, Chuck, is that money just doesn't have that all-pervading allure to me.' Hannibal puffed on his cigar, then added, 'Besides, if I really wanted a million of your dollars, I'd just get together with my associates some night and take it.'

Reaching the end of a cul-de-sac, Hannibal turned around and headed back. Carlin fumed in his seat, trying to come up with the right words to express his outrage at the situation. Several times he seemed about to speak, but he held back, each time becoming more visibly calm. Finally he nonchalantly sighed and resumed munching on his pistachios. 'Let me make you a small promise, Mr Diamond. . .provided that is your real name. . .If the Bells don't rejoin my record company under the terms of their existing contract, they'll never perform again. Not on stage and not on record.'

'Please, Mr Carlin,' Hannibal yawned. 'It's a little late in the game for idle threats.'

'I'm not an idle man,' Carlin proclaimed. 'You'll see that I mean business. I believe the ladies are scheduled to do a show at the Greek Theatre tomorrow night?'

'That's right, jack,' B.A. said.

'My name is not Jack, and that engagement will not take place,' Carlin insisted.

'Sure it will,' Hannibal countered. 'And none of the proceeds are going to end up flowing your way either, my friend.'

Back near the heavy equipment, Face and Murdock had herded the Cardenac brothers inside the milk truck and then covered the entire vehicle with a heavy tarp. Hannibal pulled to a stop alongside the truck and told Face, 'Nice job, guys. Too bad we didn't bring any ribbons or bows.'

Carlin finished the last of his pistachios and crumpled the empty bag in his large hands. From the look on his face it was clear that he wished he could dispense with Hannibal as easily. 'We have challenged each other,' he told his captor. 'All that remains now is to see who wins. I have other appointments at the moment, though, so if you would be so kind as to get out of my car and take your bodyguard with you. . .'

'Am I missing something here, Chuck?' Hannibal inquired. 'Seems to me we're the ones holding the guns on you.'

Carlin laughed jovially. 'What are you going to do, Mr Diamond? Kidnap me. . .kill me? I don't think so. You see, despite all your reckless accusations, I have a clean record and an army of lawyers to make sure I stay that way. You couldn't pin anything on me in Miami Beach, and I run things just as carefully out here and in Chicago. You'd be a fool to harm me, and while you might be a lot of other things, I'll have to concede that you're not foolish.'

'So much flattery, I can hardly stand it.' Hannibal nodded at Murdock, who went around and opened the front door on Carlin's side of the vehicle. Hannibal told Carlin, 'Get out of the car, Chuck.'

'Really. . .' Carlin scoffed.

'Yeah, really!' B.A. yelled, reaching over the front seat to jerk Carlin out into Murdock's waiting arms.

Murdock applied a full nelson on the obese man long enough for B.A. to get out of the Charger and bind Carlin's hands and feet with lengths of heavy-duty cable. As Baracus shoved Carlin up next to the tarp-draped van, Face headed off into the darkness long enough to retrieve something from the trunk of his Corvette, parked some fifty yards downhill, near a runoff culvert. When he returned, he was carrying a professional-sized paint sprayer and a bucket of paint.

'Hey, what's going on here?' Carlin wanted to know.

'I suspect you've had things pretty much your way all your life, Mr Carlin,' Hannibal said as he helped Face hook up the sprayer to the bucket. 'We thought it'd be nice to arrange for you to experience an abject lesson in humility.'

'What!??'

'Yes, I know it's probably a word you haven't heard much, Chuck, but you'll remember it real quick.'

'Let me go, you worthless swine!'

'Now, now, sticks and stones, Chuck.' Face chided.

Hannibal manned the paint sprayer and took a step forward, pointing the nozzle at Carlin as he asked, 'You ever had the blues, hmm? I don't think so, but we'll take care of that for you, right about now. . .'

Activating the sprayer, Hannibal sent a steady flow of blue paint rushing out at Carlin, covering him and the tarp he was standing in front of.

'I think mebbe he's gonna need two coats,' B.A. sneered from the sidelines as he watched. 'I told you we shoulda bought some primer!'

'Don't worry, Chuck,' Hannibal said as he sprayed the last few pints on his nemesis. 'It's latex. A couple dozen showers ought to take most of it off.'

'I'll get you for this!' Carlin wailed blindly, afraid to open his eyes.

'Give us your best shot, Chuck ol' boy,' Hannibal encouraged. 'We'll be waiting.'

As the rest of the Team started heading off into the darkness, Murdock sidled up next to the milktruck and shouted through the tarp, 'All your guns are in the portojohn by the big bulldozer. You might need a snorkle mask when you go swimming for 'em, though. . .'

A fresh blast of curses steamed out of the truck as Murdock rushed off to join his comrades. They were all taking long strides toward the culvert, where their vehicles were barely visible in the blackened shadows.

'That was a nice touch with the paint, Hannibal,' Face conceded, 'but why paint him blue?'

'I couldn't find green,' Hannibal said.

'That's not what I mean.'

As they carefully headed down the steep sides of the culvert, Hannibal explained, 'Carlin's the kind of guy who never does his own dirty work. I wanted to get him so mad that he'd get in on the end of this caper personally. That way, when the net drops, he'll be in it with the others and we'll be able to give the cops plenty to hang on him.'

Back up the hill, Hannibal's plan was taking shape nicely. Moments after Antonio Cardenac burst through the tarp and began wiping paint out of Carlin's eyes, the crime boss roared, 'They've taken me for a fool, but I'll show them! They'll regret the day they ever crossed Charles Carlin!'

'We'll take care of them next time, sir,' Antonio vowed. 'You have my word on it!'

'You can help me all you want,' Carlin said, 'but this time I'm taking charge personally of their execution. . .'

31

The following afternoon, The Bells were onstage at the Greek Theatre, one of Los Angeles' more prestigious concert auditoriums. Roadies and technicians were roaming about, setting up equipment and doing sound checks while the four women practised their moves and harmonies for that night's scheduled performance. The A-Team was on hand, too, carefully scrutinising the movements of everyone in the outdoor amphitheatre. Hannibal was checking the hills surrounding the facility through binoculars when Face climbed up the aisle steps and came over to join him.

'Let me have a look through those, Hannibal.'

Hannibal handed the binoculars over. He seemed puzzled. 'I don't get it. It's too calm around here. Too quiet.'

'You gotta be kidding,' Face said as he slowly pivoted in place, peering through the magnifying lenses, 'That guy who's tuning the guitar sounds like a one-man heavy metal band.'

'I'm talking about Carlin. He hasn't played his hand yet, and it's been over twelve hours since we gave him that blue tan.'

'Maybe he's still soaking in a tub full of mineral spirits,' Face speculated. 'Anyway, I think. . .well, well, well. . .

what do we have here?'

'Got something?' Hannibal asked, looking in the direction Face had the binoculars pointed.

'Yessiree, I've definitely found something worth getting a closer look at.' Face was focusing on the stage, where the four women were dancing in synch, wearing tube tops and high-cut shorts.

'I should have known,' Hannibal mused. He lit up a cigar and looked over the vacant stands, still troubled. 'You know, Face, I was figuring they'd never let us even get the girls close to the theatre. Now that they're here, they can stay in their dressing rooms until tonight and it's going to be damn difficult for Carlin to keep 'em off the stage.'

Once Face had had a good eyeful of The Bells, he lowered the binoculars. 'Do you think we've been had?'

Hannibal shook his head. 'Something's going on here. I wish I knew what it was.'

Using arm signals, Hannibal waved across the amphitheatre to Murdock and B.A., who were watching the parking lot from the bowl's upper rim. B.A. signalled back that they hadn't seen anything of a suspicious nature. After Hannibal motioned back for Murdock to move over and cover their territory, he and Face headed down the steps to the stage area.

The women were finishing up their practice number, and as soon as they stopped, a stage manager appeared from behind the speaker banks and called out, 'Miss King, there's a call for you in the dressing room. Some guy who says it's urgent.'

'This might be it,' Hannibal said as he jumped up onto the stage and followed Charlotte back to the dressing room. Face remained behind with the other women, clearly enjoying the responsibility.

The dressing room was brightly lit and filled with a variety of gowns and other costumes that would be worn by The Bells during their performance. Charlotte hurried by a vase filled with roses that Hannibal had bought for the women and picked up the phone.

'This is Charlotte.'

'Miss King. . .' It was Charles Carlin's oily voice that oozed into her ear. 'I have your brother with me. Would you like to talk to him?'

'Billy?' Charlotte gasped. 'You have Billy?'

'Yes, you could say we drafted him during football practice this afternoon,' Carlin laughed lightly. 'Of course, he can't play that well at the moment. You see, he's tied up, so to speak. . .'

'How dare you!' Charlotte shouted into the receiver. 'He better not be harmed!'

'Oh, he's fine. . .for the time being,' Carlin assured her. 'Here, I'll even let you talk to him.'

After a few seconds, Billy's voice came on the line, sounding high-pitched and nervous. 'Charlotte, they kidnapped me! Right at the school!'

'Billy! Are you all right?'

Carlin's voice came back over the line. 'See, he's in fine shape, and there's no reason why he can't stay that way.'

'What do you want?' Charlotte said, her eyes beginning to tear. Hannibal tapped her on the shoulder and took the phone from her as he patted her on the back to comfort her.

'I know you're in the middle of rehearsals, but maybe we can still squeeze in a few minutes to work out our new five-year contract.'

'I gotta hand it to ya, Chuckie,' Hannibal said. 'You stooped lower than I thought.'

'I assure you, if the need calls for it, I can be so low I can walk under an alligator's belly with my hat on,' Carlin said. 'You might also be interested in knowing that if I don't get my way, this poor boy is going to get rubbed out just as surely as that damn paint you sprayed on me last night.'

'Those are mighty stiff terms,' Hannibal said. With his free hand, Hannibal quickly scribbled a note on the vanity mirror with a tube of lipstick. 'HAVE FACE TRACE CALL.'

'You had your chance to settle this thing and you blew it,' Carlin taunted. 'Now, instead of a million bucks, you'll get nothin' but this kid! What's more, you're gonna have to void your power of attorney over The Bells and give me full rein over 'em, just like it was before you stuck your nose in my business.'

Charlotte hastened out of the room as Hannibal tried to play for time. 'When's this all supposed to happen, Chuck?'

'Griffith Park. Six-thirty tonight. We'll bring Billy, you bring The Bells. Come alone. If you play along fair and square, you guys can go back to the Greek and go on for The Bells, maybe sing some Barber Shop Quartet.'

'And if we don't?'

'If you don't, this boy dies, pure and simple. Think about it.'

Face rushed into the dressing room, rummaging through B.A.'s kit of gadgets, trying to find something he could use to tap the line and trace Carlin's call. Hannibal thought fast and told Carlin, 'Well, you know, Chuck, I've been giving a lot of thought to that offer of yours last night, and I—'

'That was a one-time-only offer and you passed on it, pal,' Carlin said. 'You only have one choice now and time is wasting. Goodbye!'

'Wait. . .!'

A dial tone buzzed in Hannibal's ear and he slowly set down the phone. Charlotte returned to the room, weeping openly.

'They're going to kill my brother! We have to do what they say. Anything! Cancel the concert, sign a contract, I don't care!'

'Easy, Charlotte, easy,' Hannibal said as Face bleakly set down the satchel beside him. 'It's going to turn out okay. You girls go on and get ready for the show. I guarantee that we'll have Billy back here, safe and sound, before the curtain goes up.'

'How?' Charlotte demanded. 'How are you going to do that?'

'I don't know yet,' Hannibal confessed, 'but I'll think of something. . .'

32

In the time it took Face to summon Murdock and B.A. and brief them on the sudden change of events, Hannibal had made arrangements with the theatre management to beef up security around the stage and dressing room. As The A-Team strode hastily out to the parking lot and their waiting van, Hannibal was giving his grey matter a good workout, trying to improvise a new plan.

'Our first problem is to find out where they are,' he thought out loud.

'Hey, that's no problem, Hannibal,' B.A. said.

'How's that B.A.?'

'When you were drivin' Carlin around last night, I slipped a bug under the back seat,' B.A. said as he unlocked the van. 'All we gotta do is tune in and if they're usin' that crazy Charger, we're in!'

Hannibal slapped B.A. on the back as the others climbed into the van. 'Now that's what I call incentive! Good job, B.A.!'

'Lemme get this straight,' Murdock said, taking Hannibal's customary spot in the front of the van. 'My hero, the Baracian One, exhibited an incredible feat of prescience. He anticipated a need and filled it. The man foresaw the future! Such vision! It boggles the mind, I'm tellin' ya!'

'Come on, Murdock, will you knock it off?' Face moaned.

As he started up the engine, B.A. looked back at Face and Hannibal. 'I don't know how come you guys are always pickin' on Murdock. The man ain't so bad.'

Hannibal and Face simultaneously muttered, 'Huh?'

'Okay, so the man's a little. . .unconventional, but he's got some good ideas, so leave him be, dig?'

'I'm hallucinating,' Face guessed, holding his wrist out to Hannibal. 'Quick, check my pulse. B.A. is actually talking up Murdock?'

Murdock was in heaven. He clapped his hands and rubbed his palms together as B.A. pulled out of the parking lot. 'Are we a groovy, happening bunch of guys here, or what?'

Face drowned out Murdock's euphoria by turning up the homing meter and filling the van with the raucous crackle of static, through which a faint bleeping sounded. Interpreting the signal, Face called out directions, and as soon as the van was heading west on the northbound Ventura Freeway the bleep grew louder in proportion to the fading of the static.

'Must be back at the housing development,' Face said when the signal continued to grow stronger as they cut through the lower part of the San Fernando Valley. However, when they reached the Mullholland/Valley Circle Drive turnoff, it became clear that their destination was not north at all, but rather to the southwest.

B.A. drove over the freeway and past the Motion Picture Hospital and Retirement Home, then linked up with Mullholland Drive, a winding two-lane country road that followed the spine of the Santa Monica Mountains. Lavish estates and quasi-mansions, most of them only a few years old, stood out at regular intervals, intruding upon the hearty chaparral and manzanita that grew in abundance where it hadn't been cleared away by developers. By degrees, the signal continued to grow stronger, luring The A-Team deeper into the canyon country. Fewer and fewer houses came into view.

'Man, where are we goin?' B.A. complained as he wrestled with the steering wheel to handle the countless hairpin turns the roadway took. 'This looks like where them TV hillbillies came from before they moved to Beverly Hills!'

'Just keep driving and don't take any shortcuts down these cliffs,' Hannibal said, peering out the window at a precipitous drop-off a mere few feet away from the shoulder of the road.

After passing around a jutting knob of a small mountain, the Team came in sight of Malibu Lake, a manmade body of water tucked away in the heart of the mountains and surrounded by older, quainter homes. However, the signal emanating from the planted transmitter wasn't coming from that community, either, but from somewhere still further to the west.

'Okay, start slowing down,' Face said as B.A. drove past another stretch of road flanked by new homes, most of them unfinished. The meter was putting out a clear bleeping now, with virtually no conflicting static.

'There's the Dodge!' Murdock suddenly cried out, pointing through the windshield at a Tudor-style mansion set back a good fifty yards from the road, on a lot green with freshly-laden sod. The White Charger was parked up near the front entrance in a horseshoe driveway. A white picket fence surrounded the property, which was divided into a lawn area, riding grounds for a handful of horses, and a plot of farming ground that looked freshly tilled.

B.A. drove past the house and pulled off the road at a spot where the manzanita crept out almost as far as the curb, providing good cover.

'Okay,' Hannibal said once the engine was silenced. 'They aren't going to be expecting us, so we have the element of surprise in our favour. They have the home court advantage, so I figure we're going into this about even. That's not good enough for me. We need more of an edge. Murdock, I want you and your big buddy to find a way into that barn at the back corner of the property. See if you can find something of use to shake 'em up. Face, take the fifty-calibre and set up shop on the west end. There's a big stone gateway there that should give you plenty of cover.'

'What are you going to do?' Face asked Hannibal.

As Hannibal opened a large trunk in the back of the van and began sifting through his make-up kit and various disguises, he told Face and the others, 'There's only one proper way to deliver the kind of message we want to send to our good friend Mr Carlin. . .'

33

'Well, it's getting to be that time,' Carlin said, inspecting the jewel-studded watch strapped to his pudgy wrist. He swilled down the last of his bourbon and branch water, then smacked his lips as he guided his weighty frame out of the rocking chair he had been sitting in. Almost as an afterthought, he reached out to the chess board set before him and manoeuvred a rook to the opposite corner. 'Checkmate, Talbot.'

Talbot Black, owner of the ranch and Carlin's west coast business partner, was a thin, balding man whose hornrimmed glasses gave him the look of a university professor rather than a cut-throat entrepreneur. He puffed casually on his briar pipe as he contemplated the board, then conceded, 'Well done, Charles, I must say.'

They were in the study of the newly-built Tudor mansion, which was adorned with a variety of artworks playing off a fox-hunting motif. Besides the two men, the Cardenac brothers were also present, standing like matched chess pieces on either side of Billy Rey, who was tied to a chair.

'Let's hope your friends value your hide, young man,' Carlin told Billy as he signalled for Antonio and Louis to untie the youth from the chair.

'Why are you doing this?' Billy asked. 'You already have tons of money. Why do you have to get so hot and bothered about my sister's group?'

'It's a matter of principle, son. I'm a man of diverse interests, and I try to treat them all with equal concern. If I were to start getting lacksadaisical about one investment, it'd be a bad sign. Empires fall when the weak links aren't tended to. You should remember that. I'm teaching you a very valuable lesson here.'

'Yeah, well, I hope The A-Team teaches *you* a lesson!' Billy snapped as Antonio Cardenac pulled him up out of the chair.

'The who?'

'My friends. They'll take care of you.'

'The A-Team, The A-Team. . .' When Carlin was finally able to place the name, a sickly smile came to his face. 'So that's who Diamond Management really is. I should have suspected as much. But, it's of no consequence. They might rate an "A" for effort, but when all's said and done, I'm afraid they're not going to be much more than a C-Team. . .Antonio, Louis, take Billy out to the milk truck for our next delivery. I'll follow in the Charger.'

Carlin and Black exchanged a final quick farewell, then Carlin headed out the side door to his parked Dodge. The rest of the Sicilian gang was standing guard at various points around the house, and while Vincent and Joseph joined the Cardenac brothers in the milk truck, Dom and Rico got into the Charger with their boss.

The milk truck rolled to a stop in front of the main entrance, and Louis got out to open the gate. As he was doing so, a hunchbacked mailman trudged up from the road, sagging under the weight of his leather totebag. He managed a grin under his weathered red moustache as he greeted Louis. 'Howdy do. Gotta special delivery here fer a Mr Carlin. Y'all think ya kin sign fer it?'

'I'm in a hurry, old man,' Louis said coldly as he swung the gate door open.

'Well, hell's bells, son, that's the whole dang trouble with folks nowadays,' the mailman complained as he withdrew a clipboard from the mail pouch. 'Always rushin' this way an' that. Lookie here, all I need's yer John Hancock and then I can turn the goods over and be on me way. Won't take ye but a second, now, will it?'

'All right, all right!'

As Louis grabbed the clipboard and chased an inky scrawl across the register with a pen, he asked the mailman, 'What's the package, anyway?'

'Some kinda religious artefact.' The mailman suddenly lashed out with his fist, catching Louis under the chin and crumpling the Sicilian into an unconscious heap. 'I think it was a right cross.'

As Hannibal ripped off his moustache and yanked out an Uzi submachine gun from his delivery bag, Face stood up behind the gateway and blasted out the front end of the milk truck with his automatic rifle.

While Antonio, Vincent, and Joseph were reacting to this unsuspected seige, Billy saw his chance for escape and lunged headlong out the side door of the milktruck. Even though his arms were tied behind his back, he was still agile enough to land on his feet and scramble out the gateway, avoiding the whizz of bullets coming at him and Hannibal.

'Get behind the gate with Face!' Hannibal shouted at Billy as he charged the milk truck, blowing out the windows with his Uzi and gaining the drop on the Sicilians trapped inside before they could get at their weapons.

Carlin witnessed the assault from behind the wheel of his Charger, and rather than join in the fray, he shifted the car into reverse and started speeding backwards down the dirt road leading to the farming acreage and the big barn.

Face pulled out his walkie-talkie as he rushed to help Hannibal apprehend the men in the milktruck. Putting the mouthpiece to his lips, he shouted, 'You got company comin' your way, B.A.!'

Carlin pulled off onto the grass and spun his Dodge around, then raced past the barn on his way to the open fields past the nearest picket fence. Before he could make good his escape, however, the side wall of the barn exploded outwards and a massive tractor broadsided the Charger, sending it crashing into a stack of bundled hay.

'Way to go, oh Baracian One!' Murdock cheered, rushing out of the barn and waving to B.A., who was at the controls of the tractor.

B.A. looked over his shoulder, where he could see Face and Hannibal leading their captives out of the milktruck, then turned back to the battered Charger and grinned. 'Yeah, we got quite a harvest here!'

Murdock kicked the front end of the Dodge as he waved a gun at Carlin and his two underlings. 'Yeah, a real bumper crop!'

Epilogue

The benefit concert by The Bells came off without a hitch and proved to be a major success, drawing a capacity crowd for what most critics declared to be the group's most inspired performance in their young career. The A-Team was there, along with Billy Rey, cheering the women on from the backstage area. Following the concert, there was a celebration dinner party held at Ma Maison, and when the talk turned away from The Bells and the imprisonment of their former management team, the main topic of discussion was the upcoming return of St Mary's Academy to the gridiron. During the two days The A-Team had been away, Sister Catherine and a few of the other nuns had supervised practice sessions to make sure that the team wouldn't go rusty before the season premiere, and there were high hopes that St Mary's would come up with a stunning upset against Banning High.

Some things, however, were even beyond the scope of The A-Team's prowess. Going into the final quarter of the big game, the home team crowd at St Mary's field was in dismal spirits, and the scoreboard told the whole story. Banning was routing the orphans by a score of 46-0.

Billy Rey was putting up a valiant effort, having gained over a hundred yards with a combination of passes and runs, but he had lost even more yardage on plays when Banning maulers crushed through the offensive line and dragged him down before he could get off a pass, or break free for an end run. When he was brought down for still another five-yard loss, Face grimaced on the sidelines, fighting a losing battle to remain optimistic in the wake of his team's brutal demise.

'It's okay!' he shouted to the youths as they drew into a huddle. 'It's okay. Hang tough! Keep at 'em! It's not over yet!'

A few feet away from Face, B.A. was viewing the proceedings with no pretence of good cheer. He looked mean and angry and fed-up. Turning to Face, he said, 'Tell your guys to block, man! Billy can't do nothin' when he's got half of Banning's team chargin' down his throat!'

Face rolled his eyes and looked pleadingly at Hannibal and Murdock, who sat on the bench, trying not to get overly involved in the feud between their associates. 'Hannibal, can you believe this grief I'm hearing from a guy whose defence allowed forty-six points in three quarters?'

'Leave me out of it, Face,' Hannibal said. 'I'm just the equipment manager around here.'

'And I'm just a trainer,' Murdock said, 'although I might have to take some drastic measures if the tide doesn't turn around here soon.'

St Mary's punted and Banning returned the kick for still another touchdown, further fanning the fires between Face and B.A..

'This is getting painful, Murdock,' Hannibal murmured. 'I think maybe I'm gonna bow out and go up in the stands to check on the ladies.'

'I know what you mean, Colonel,' Murdock replied, wringing a towel in his hands. 'Knute Rockne. . .Vince Lombari. . .they would have had some inspiration for their players at half-time. B.A., he didn't say nothin'. He just glared. I mean, in 1942, Notre Dame was down and almost out. . .it was half-time and Knute Rockne told 'em the story of Frank Gipp. Have you heard that story, Hannibal?'

'Everybody's heard that story, Murdock.' Hannibal ran his fingers through his hair and adjusted his shirt as he stood up and looked into the stands. The Bells were a few rows up, and they waved at Hannibal, gesturing for him to join them. 'Well, since this case *is* over, I think we can indulge ourselves in a little extracurricular activity, don't you think?'

Murdock was still riding his own train of thought, however, and he railed on, 'The Rock got 'em together, Hannibal. He told 'em how the Gipper played a game with pneumonia and how he died on the field. . .' Murdock coughed and changed his voice into what was supposed to be an impersonation of Pat O'Brien playing Knute Rockne. '"When Notre Dame is down, and when you really need a win. . ."'

'Murdock, spare me, please!'

'"Gather the boys together and tell 'em. . .win one for the Gipper!"' Murdock began to sniff, moved to tears by his soliloquy. Hannibal reached into his pocket for a handkerchief and handed it to his weeping comrade.

'Here, Murdock,' he said. 'Help yourself. I'm gonna go up in the stands and see if I can't win one for the Hannibal!'

As Hannibal moved off, Murdock blew his nose and stared out at the field, where the St Mary's offence was getting ready to make yet another desperate drive to put some points on the scoreboard. A flash of inspiration sparked in Murdock's eyes, and the moment Billy took the snap and back-pedalled for a pass, the weeping trainer bolted out onto the training field, screaming, 'I got it! I got it! I'm gonna score for ya, Gip! I'm gonna win one for ya!'

'What's he doing?' Face exclaimed as he saw Murdock pursue Billy Rey's pass and intercept it before it was about to land in the waiting arms of another St Mary's player.

'The fool's gone cuckoo on me again!' B.A. howled as he started running down the sidelines.

Dodging Banning and St Mary's players alike, Murdock ran a pattern that would have made Crazy Legs Hirsch dizzy, and finally ended up in the end zone, where he spiked the ball into the turf and did a quick dance before turning to face the bewildered audience in the stands. His face was streaming with tears of emotion.

'There ya go, Gipper! There ya go! This one's for you!'

Murdock's one-man celebration ended abruptly when B.A. blindsided him from behind and the two men tumbled onto the grass.

'What the hell you doin', fool?' B.A. demanded as he got back up to his feet.

Murdock remained seated on the turf, pouting at his former idol. 'I thought you could coach, B.A.! I thought you had something. I thought you could mould men. But no, you couldn't even give 'em the Gipper speech! You didn't call 'em a buncha girls. You didn't do none of the great Knute Rockne stuff! You just stood there looking like a played-out gold mine, reflecting the light and looking stupid!'

'I'll show you some Knute Rockne stuff!' B.A. warned. 'I'll drop kick your butt inta the next county!'

'Whaddya mean? I'm the only guy who scored!'

B.A. charged Murdock, who quickly leapt to his feet. A buzzer sounded, announcing the end of the game, and as the players left the field, B.A. and Murdock began a hundred yard dash, with the latter having a slight edge due to the amount of gold B.A. had to carry with him.

Up in the stands, Hannibal cheered his associates on, surrounded by the four members of The Bells. He was toking grandly on a fat cigar and loving the attention he was getting. 'Now that Diamond Management is handling your career,' he cracked, 'I suggest some high-level huddles to talk future multi-pic packs. We'll confab at Ah Fong's, ink a deal and go boffo at the ticket booths!'

'What?' Charlotte asked.

'Agent talk,' Hannibal explained. 'It's confusing, sure, but I got the rap down pat. How about it, girls?'

'Well,' Jennifer admitted, 'we did agree to turn over ten percent of our income as payment for all you've done for us. . .'

'Good, then it's settled!'

Face trudged up the aisle and stared forlornly at Hannibal. 'I'm down there being humiliated and you're up here partying. It isn't fair, Hannibal!'

'Who said life was fair?' Hannibal laughed. 'Hey, leave your number, maybe I'll get back to you.'

Down on the field, Murdock lengthened the distance between himself and B.A., then cut sideways and headed up into the stands. He sought out Hannibal, crying, 'You gotta save me from the big guy! He wants to turn me into a six-foot pig skin!'

'Aw, come on, Murdock,' Hannibal scoffed. 'You don't really think the Baracian One would harm you, do you?'

'Baracian One nuthin'!' Murdock whimpered, cowering behind Hannibal and the women as B.A. stormed up the steps. 'He's nothin' but one angry mudsucker! You're the boss, Hannibal. Tell him to cool off!'

Hannibal grinned. 'The Boss. I like that. Yeah, I just love it when a plan comes together. . .'